The One and Only
Fat Chance

PLEASE NOTE:
If you require any trigger warnings,
please refer to the note at the end of the book
on page 208.

THE ONE AND ONLY FAT CHANCE

Copyright © 2023 by Mark Brennan

Published in the United States by the Fullery Free Press

All rights reserved. Printed and published for eBook in the United States of America. For information, address Fullery Free Press, 1101 Balmoral Drive, Cary, NC 27511.
Inquiries can also be sent to info@fulleryfreepress.com.

www.fulleryfreepress.com

Interior formatted by Ryan Forsythe
Cover art by Savannah Brennan

First Fullery Free Press Paperback Edition: June 2023
Print ISBN-13: 979-8-9885319-0-6
Ebook ISBN-13: 979-8-9885319-1-3

Fullery Free Press
CARY, NC

For the woman who said *test*

The One and Only
Fat Chance

W̲HAT'S IN A NAME?

Well, if you ask me, a whole hell of a lot. But I also believe we all have two names—the one we're given at birth, and the one we make for ourselves. If we're fortunate enough, we'll find that they're one and the same. The rest of us might not have it so easy.

My parents named me Chance Lee Branch. The disadvantages in my life started the moment that first name was printed onto my birth certificate—which also documented my birth weight of thirteen pounds, eight ounces, distributed across a length of twenty-one inches. I was a fat baby. And I'd stay that way.

Therefore I was born, and fated to forever be, Fat Chance.

I learned the euphemism *fat chance*—a facetious term for severely unfavorable odds—well after it became my moniker. When kids on the playground in second grade started calling me that, I assumed it to be just another cruel slur—something I'd already grown accustomed to. My name is Chance, and I'm fat; thus they called me Fat Chance. Seemed simple enough.

It wasn't until years later that I overheard one of the talking heads during Dad's steady dose of all-day cable news shouting my name in argument. "Fat Chance!" one angry face yelled at another. My head whipped around at the TV, thinking for a moment I might be famous. But of course, I wasn't.

Not yet, anyway.

The troubles with my name weren't limited to this nasty variation I'd never escape. In addition to being eponymously overweight, I have a terrible longitudinal lisp (an affliction which, ironically, is nearly impossible for me to pronounce). Years of speech therapy and a lingual surgical procedure could dampen it only so much before I realized I had to just deal with it. So, when I introduce myself, it sounds like I'm saying my name is *Thanthsh. Thanthsh Branthsh.* Go ahead and try it— stick your tongue out and say my name.

Exactly.

As soon as I started drinking—which, under the circumstances, was age thirteen—pronouncing my name reached a new level of difficulty. After a few beers, my speech became intelligible only to those familiar with my unique dialect. After a case or so, I couldn't even understand myself.

I tried to give myself some less hurtful nicknames, but I found that self-assigning a nickname is pretty much impossible. Flattering names like *Big Chief* or *Heavy C* just don't appeal much to savage grade-schoolers. Later on, I tried going by my middle name, but got the same result. Why call a guy Lee when he'll respond just as readily to Fat Chance? Even my dad refused, saying he hated the name Lee. In a drunken haze, he once revealed they'd given me that middle name out of delirium after my mom's marathon, potentially life-threatening labor and delivery.

It was hard to decide which was worse between my name and my size. I think I'd have been okay with everyone calling me Fat Chance, and introducing myself as *Thanthsh Branthsh,* if I could've just been a little less noticeable. Understand, by the start of junior year I grew to be a whopping 440 pounds, towering over literally everyone I'd ever met at six feet, ten inches tall. It'd always been impossible not to attract the stare of every set of eyes, in every single room I entered. That kind of attention had never appealed to me. Even if I were that big and super sexy, I'd still wish it away.

But sexy, I was not. Not only did the Good Lord bless me with a body too big for the cruel world, as well as an unsayable name, but He also endowed me with curly copper hair and a dense spattering of freckles that make me look permanently flushed. This only worsens after exposure to the sun (which, in southern Missouri, is unavoidable). And since my parents seemingly hated my presence, they always made me *play outside*, knowing full well I didn't have any friends and there was nowhere nearby to *play* besides the gravel trailer park lot and a polluted swamp beyond the rickety cattle fence. "Play *what*, exactly, Ma?" I'd always ask. "Water snakes don't follow the rules of hide-and-seek." By the end of most summers, freckles covered more of my exposed skin than the pasty white part did, making it look like I had red skin peppered with white specks.

It's also worth mentioning that all fatness is not equal. How one's excess weight is distributed has a substantial impact on self-esteem, wardrobe options, and—according to my independent observations—one's acceptance in society. When you visualize someone my size, you probably assume I'd have an enormous gut. And maybe that's accurate, relative to the next guy. But proportional to the rest of me, my belly didn't protrude much.

No—since things were so well stacked in my favor, it all had to be compensated by endowing me with perky man boobs. And not just the kind I could hide under a 4XL T-shirt—the kind that stuck out from my plump arms and belly, capped with puffy nipples visible through any material suited to the southern Missouri heat. I'd be lying if I said I never considered wearing a brassier to keep my pokies at bay. The sad truth is that I did. I tried on my mom's bra one day, but gave up on that solution only because the bra straps were painfully obvious, reshaping my body as they cut into my fat.

Oh, and let's not forget about below the waist. God forbid anything about my form be inadvertently normal, right? My *pooch*—the name I assigned to the secondary bulge below my belly—always protruded farther out than anything else, giving me the profile of a snowman constructed by overambitious children who'd chosen to challenge the laws of structural physics. The one benefit to this feature was that my pants would stay up without a belt or suspenders. I just had to nestle the waistband in the crease just so, and *bam*—I was golden.

I'm nothing if not an optimist.

My parents made me play football in high school, because going all the way back to kindergarten, other parents kept telling them I was built like a left tackle—whatever that meant. "I want *him* on my quarterback's blind side," they'd say. "The Chiefs could use him *now!*" Laughs all around from my parents and the grownups they paid attention to. I had no clue what it meant, but I gathered it meant I had value in this circle. For that reason alone, I committed to it.

When freshman year rolled around, I didn't face the possibility of missing the cut. My school was so small that any walk-on got a roster spot. And walking on was a foregone conclusion I wouldn't dare escape—it would be equivalent to a man born with gills refusing to try out for the swim team.

But even if there had been tryouts, there's no way the coaches wouldn't have made me the starting left tackle. They looked at me like a savory piece of meat when I showed up—the way a pretty woman appeared to creepy old cartoon characters. I think my parents' social lives derived mostly from people who once hoped I'd become an NFL zillionaire. But by the third game of the second season of freshman year, those hopes disappeared like farts in the wind.

I *hated* football. There was *so much running*. When we'd watch the Chiefs games on TV, the big guys didn't seem to run all that much. But that's because they don't televise the practices—which are like, twice as long as a game, and all we did was run and do other uncomfortable things the entire time. The way the position had been explained to me, I just had to keep the big guy on the other side from getting past me to tackle my quarterback. So why would I crawl like a bear when my job is just to park my big body in someone's way? When, during a game, would I ever drop to a prone position on the ground and stand up immediately to sprint in place, and then repeat such insanity? Why make me do exercises that lead to weight loss when the singular reason I'm there is that I'm the biggest player on the field?

My coaches answered legitimate questions like these with loud, harsh answers; none of which made any sense. And my fat ass wasn't here for it. To the universe's chagrin, I retired from football at age fifteen with a grand total of three sacks allowed, twenty-one penalties, and five injuries (two of which I did *not* fake!) over the course of thirteen games suited up during my freshman and sophomore years. The Chandler's Marsh Spartans (remember my lisp) were much better off without me—I'd been the worst player on the team by far. Light-years behind the next worst, Jorge Chavez, who had asthma, spoke little English, and, prior to the team orientation, had expected *fútbol* to mean *soccer*.

My parents let go of their pro football aspirations, and we all accepted that I was just a lazy, useless fatass. That was a turning point for me, I think—although not the kind a health professional or loved one would hope for. But not quite rock bottom, either, because things would certainly get worse from there.

Much worse.

I longed for my parents' acceptance. But for reasons outside my understanding, I was never good enough. They said *I love you* and all that, but it felt like lip service. A big part of me (as all parts of me are) suspected that they were ashamed or disappointed with how I turned out. Or, even more disturbing, how I was *born*. I can still remember going to playdates and hearing the other parents brag about their kids, while mine just shook their heads. Said I was a handful. I ate too much, grew out of my clothes too fast, and so on. The dent this put into our family budget seemed to be all they had to say about me.

I wasn't a child. I was livestock.

Quitting football pissed my dad off, but I was unapologetic. If he'd come to practices and seen what they put me through, I might've valued his opinion. But as it went, I felt a sense of agency. *What're you gonna do, old man?* I'd ask him in my mind. *Are you gonna force me to give a shit?*

It was the first real shift in my outlook. I sort of embraced this repugnant body of mine, even if the world never would. *I am lard ass, hear me roar*, I remember thinking—or maybe I even said it out loud. With so much weighing me down physically, I hadn't realized how heavy the burden of expectation had grown. It felt damn good to shed it, even though I knew the cost. What little worth I had to them was gone, but somehow this came with a sort of power. And I liked it.

With the death of those NFL dreams, any anticipation of my success sank from sight like the ass end of the Titanic. My parents could go back to disregarding me, and I could go back to rereading Harry Potter and Tolkien, and my favorite pastime, playing *World of Warcraft*—a multiplayer online role-playing video game where I truly mattered. At least there, my hideous form was intentional and commonplace—both on the screen and behind it.

Mom and Dad had their world, and I had mine. Dad lived and breathed his third shift mill work, and Mom did whatever she did when we weren't looking. All I knew for sure was that any and all of that was more important to them than I was. Sad as this might seem, I'd just accepted it as fact.

Socially, my brief venture in football had changed a few things. Two of the other guys on the offensive line—Seth Charles and Raymond Mack—represented the closest I'd come to actual friends, giving me at least a couple of faces to nod at as I trudged through the hallways at school. They were big dudes too, though I still dwarfed them. But they felt my pain. I know this, because I saw their faces at the end of those practices.

Seth was kind of a dick. Actually, take that back—not *kind of*. Totally. But to me, that didn't set him apart from anyone else. He called me names, mocked my lisp, punched my arm too hard, knocked books out of my hands (knowing full well the ordeal it thrust upon me to pick them up), and, my favorite, *gleeked* on me. If you're unfamiliar, *gleeking* is the bizarre ability to use the salivary glands under the tongue as gross little cannons to squirt spit at a target with disgusting range and accuracy. (God sure is a creative sadist, isn't He?) Other than being *clinically* obese (meaning barely overweight), I surmise that Seth wasn't a bad-looking dude. This made the insults cut a bit deeper when he called me ugly with that venomous expression on his face, or picked my appearance apart, flaw by endless flaw.

What made this all forgivable—commendable, even—was that Seth didn't do these things to entertain or impress others.

He did them to amuse only himself, with the same fervor and regularity regardless of who was around. And when he did it, god dammit, he looked me in the eyes. Nothing irked me more than someone ridiculing me, then basking in the public reaction instead of witnessing my hurt. *Look at what you've done to me, you coward*, I'd always think.

After football, these *gestures* slowly lessened in frequency and intensity, supplanted by actual conversation. He'd even shoot dirty looks at eavesdroppers who laughed at his jabs, as if they'd taken something that was rightfully his. By eleventh grade, I publicly referred to Seth as my friend and received no objection. This, in turn, led to me rubbing elbows with his other associates. But before this warms your heart too much, remember—Seth was a total dick.

Ray Mack was actually cool—by my criteria, anyway. To everyone else, he avoided rock bottom popularity due to my existence alone. In fact, aside from his easily pronounced name, I think the similarity of his plight to mine is what I found most endearing. While not as enormous as I was, Ray was short and pudgy, with glasses that magnified his eyeballs to three times their actual size. Instead of freckles, his face (and much of his body) was covered with constellations of pimples. He didn't have a speech impediment, but his voice cracked often, like an early pubescent boy. To augment this curse, his dream was to be a sports commentator. In his mind, he could call a game with every bit of the talent of Joe Buck, Bob Costas, or Harry Caray. The *pièce de résistance* in his catalogue of curses was a gnarly case of halitosis, propelled by his constant mouth-breathing. As bad as things got for me, there were times I wondered if he actually had it worse. Albeit, not many.

Perhaps Ray saw me the same way, because he was the only

kid at school I'd say was actually *nice* to me. He never insulted me or infringed on my personal space, let alone struck me. He laughed at my jokes and listened when I talked. He *understood* me. The problem with Ray was that he'd only behave this way in private. If even one other soul occupied the room we were in, he'd be hard-pressed to even acknowledge me.

As off-putting as I found this, part of me got it. One fatso made an easy enough target. But two, together? Not many asshole kids could withhold their cruel jokes, even if they kept them out of our earshot. I know Ray's heart sank just as much as mine at the sound of surreptitious giggling. Whatever the cruel joke, it only added insult to my intelligence that they thought I wouldn't know their stifled laughs came at my expense. So I get it—Ray was a timid guy, and I took no offense at his conditional friendship. It just sucked because the times others were around were the times I needed a friend most.

The main reason for this is that when you look, sound, and (supposedly) smell the way I do, everyone's the enemy. All humanity represents one gigantic asshole, sharing a collective asshole consciousness. The cause of this worldview isn't limited to my school's diminutive student body, either—TV, music, movies, social media, books, magazines, you name it—every form of human communication has an insatiable desire to make oversized people feel small. I've never done heroin, but based on the behavior of people who have, I can infer that it feels amazing. I'll never know what it's like to make fun of an obese person, but based on how irresistible it seems to be for others, I assume it's euphoric. Either that, or it causes great discomfort for normal-sized people to watch a heavy person walk by and not whisper, laugh, or point.

Girls don't look at a guy like me without making a face that hurts my feelings. Granted, I understand their disgust when I look in the mirror, but I don't make those hurtful faces at myself. It's hard to deduce that their repulsed looks are anything but mean-spirited. Nevertheless, I was a hormonal teenage boy. I'd often swallow my pride to look back at the most attractive of them just to get a glimpse of their perfect bodies or ornately made-up faces. Just because I'm undesirable doesn't mean I'm a eunuch.

While girls like them might've starred in my lewdest fantasies, I also had more romantic aspirations. My utopia was complicated, but an integral component of it was a girl (or woman) who could see past my physical flaws and somehow find me appealing. Sexy, even. I'd be lying if I said I never struggled to suspend my disbelief, but there were a few faces that popped up in my lucid dreams as perfect suitors.

Alanis Morissette had always been a closet crush of mine. I loved the content of her songs, but also her commentary on everything—she seemed to me like the kindest human on earth, and I adored that. And her wide, juicy lips. And her big brown eyes. This fixation stood the test of time, reaching into her less popular years when she had children and gained some weight. At that point, my infatuation accelerated into a minor obsession. She was the absolute perfect woman who could now condemn the world as I always have—from the eyes of a heavy person.

But I never fooled myself. I knew an international pop star would never be mine. And I'm not really one to be starstruck, so the next best option for my attainable dreams had to be local— slim pickings, even for a heartthrob. I won't lie—Chandler's Marsh had some good-looking girls. But I became a connoisseur of character, given my limitations on vanity, and that left a very small pool of prospects, even for fantasies.

The only girl at school I ever really had eyes on was Candace Klauss—a shy, delightfully thick classmate I'd known since grade school. I'd be lying if I said my passive fixation on her had nothing to do with her also being overweight, but it went far beyond that alone. In a way, she felt kindred—I instinctively knew that she didn't go by *Candy* because it would serve as fodder for fat jokes. I don't think I'd said more than five words to her outside of academic necessity, but if anyone from the fairer sex in our fair town could share vulnerabilities with me, I assumed it'd be her.

She also had a way with words. In math, science, and history classes over the years I'd known of her, she stayed pretty quiet. But in English classes, she transformed. Like a butterfly broken free of its chrysalis, she flaunted her true beauty. She'd use fancy words like *homogenous* and *levity* in discussions about books we were supposed to have read, and show her raw self for those audiences alone. When we'd have to read Shakespeare, she spoke the dialect as if it were her native tongue. In the occasional years I shared an English class with her, I felt like I had tickets to the hottest show in town. In that perfect setting, she bucked all expectations and came out of her shell on command. I envied her for that.

Heartening as this may be, I never found the nerve over the years to talk to her, let alone gush about what an ambassador she'd become for the socially underprivileged. *Someday*, I'd tell myself as I tried to fall asleep. Someday, a companion like her won't be too much to ask for.

At least, not in my dreams.

THE WORLD IS INFESTED WITH PEOPLE WHO MAKE TARGETS out of people like me. So when I walked out the door each day, I fought through a fortification of adversaries bent on breaking my spirit. But just like excess weight, all enemies are not equal. While they do often seem to blend together in one, *homogenous* horde of emotional barbarians, some of them stand on a pedestal above the crowd and shout in a heroic voice, "Behold! I am king of all assholes!" For me, that King of Assholes was a kid named Chip Smith. *Of course* his name would make me spit—both figuratively and literally.

I can honestly say that, despite the years of abuse, I'd never considered killing anyone—including myself. Life is hard, but I never wished to end it with suicide or life behind bars for murder. I enjoyed the simple pleasures: delicious food, video games, fantasy novels, and comic books. They made life worth living.

That all changed junior year, when Chip Smith came to the school.

Looking back, I should've known he hid his own torment. People don't behave with wanton asshole-ness unless they're driven to. But on the surface, I didn't see it—I doubt anyone did. Chip seemed to have it all. He was tall and chiseled, with flawless skin and eyebrows, and a mop of dirty blond hair that probably fell into perfect position the moment his head rose from the pillow. His voice was silky and baritone, and he had teeth so white and straight, I suspected they were dentures—and I'd yearned to one day prove it by yanking them out of his pretty face. I always asked myself why someone who had so much going for him would treat people like me the way he did.

The problem was that I never really tried to answer that question.

Because like everyone else, I understand my own pain most of all. And Chip delivered more than enough of it to kill my empathy for him. From my elevated vantage point at the other end of my high school's only hallway, I could see he was bad news the day he walked through the doors. My first clue was how the girls fawned and whispered to each other as he walked by—high school girls gravitate to assholes with uncanny accuracy. It's a law of social physics.

The next warning sign was the instant he caught sight of me. He didn't make the faintest effort to mask his shock at my image—in fact, he exaggerated it. I couldn't hear what he said as he pointed at me, but it didn't matter. The reaction it got from everyone else delivered the cruelest words to ever resonate inside my head.

I've had it easy until now.

When you envision bullying, what comes to mind is probably something akin to the way Seth, my second-best friend (out of two), treated me. Slapstick assaults, verbal degradation, intermittent little reminders that I'm powerless and unwanted—you know, the basics. I have to believe (dare I say hope?) that very few people in the world have been acquainted with what the next level of bullying looks like, which is what Chip brought into the equation in October of eleventh grade. And when I say *next level*, it's under the assumption the level above *that* is what drug cartels and terrorist organizations do to people.

I endured a month of erratic severity in his antics. Once, he secured my locker with his own padlock—fair play, from my vantage point. He got three days of in-school suspension for shooting me point-blank in the eyeball with a large rubber band. He'd originally been threatened with expulsion and criminal charges, since my pathetic howl caught the attention of the school resource officer. The punishment got reduced significantly when he claimed it was an accident—that he'd meant to shoot my arm, and missed. The principal even asked me to vouch for him, and to my own shame, I did. Believe me, I considered divulging what a monster he was. But if it didn't guarantee his expulsion, it wasn't worth the risk. He'd make me pay. I decided to take my lumps and hope he'd be deterred by his slap on the wrist.

The unpredictability of Chip's early attacks traumatized me. And I'm not being hyperbolic—my therapist would eventually diagnose me with PTSD. And when I say *unpredictable*, I don't mean he put me off guard with his timing. I mean I never knew how far he'd go—he made it clear on Halloween that year that even felonious behavior wasn't out of bounds.

Nothing was.

Then, costumed as Billy the Kid, he caught me alone in the bathroom.

I'd been taking my usual after-lunch dump in the stall when I heard him come in with his band of merry assholes. He recognized my enormous shoes and made farting noises with his hands, and the kind of bathroom jokes you'd expect from someone half his age. When they all left, I made the mistake of thinking the coast was clear, and emerged to wash my hands. I'd zoned out at the sink, considering whether I wanted to stomach a glance at myself in the mirror, when Chip came back in alone, shutting the heavy wooden door behind him. (Until then, I'd never even realized there was a door to close. This only compounded my shock.)

He stopped just in front of me, gazing up at me with a smirk that would look friendly to a casual observer. In the same tone he'd use to ask me where I got my pants, he said, "Why are you still alive?"

I snorted. "Uh, I dunno? I guess 'cause I haven't died yet?"

"Don't you think you should?"

"Umm—*no?*"

He squinted, disgusted that I didn't get it. "Nobody likes you, fatass. Your parents don't love you, you don't have any friends . . . just *look at you.* What could you possibly have to live for?"

I shrugged.

"If I was you, I'd kill myself."

My face got hot. I considered lunging at him, or trampling him, or crushing him against the wall, but risking his retaliation wasn't a breaking point I'd reached yet. Speed wasn't my thing, and if I missed, I'd be toast. So I just tried to get through the moment.

"I bet you would," I said.

Chip lifted up his tattered white button-down shirt to reveal his gym-ad abs, obstructed by the ivory handle of a large revolver. He drew it and rested it on his shoulder, aimed at the ceiling. It looked fake, like a prop you'd see in a western—but by its obvious bulk, I knew it was very real. He wasn't just dressed as Billy the Kid; he was in full method actor mode. I heard him lock the hammer back just before he leveled the nickel-plated barrel at my face. He used an authentic cowboy drawl. "I could do it for you, if you like."

Instinctively, I raised both palms and shook my head. I could feel him looking at my jostling extra chins. He looked ready to laugh, but caught himself. After a few seconds of paralyzed silence, I found my words. "No, thank you."

He turned the gun sideways, nudging it closer to my face. "Here. *You* do it." His face betrayed no concern that I'd take the gun and use it against him, despite the ease with which I could. "Probably takes a pretty big slug to put a hole through a head fat as yours, but this here's a .44 Magnum, boy. It'll do the trick just fine. Don't worry—you won't feel a thing."

"I'm good," I said.

"Take the gun, fatass. Don't you wanna kill *me*, at least? I know you'd like to kill one of us. Go on, take it!"

As he pushed it even closer to me, I gave it another thought. But before that thought finished, loud coughing emitted from outside the door—contrived coughing. Chip let the hammer down and holstered the weapon in his waistline with a deftness that told me this wasn't his first time handling it. A split second later, the door swung open and in walked Mr. Foley, the history teacher.

He interrogated us about what we were up to, passively accusing us of vaping or doing drugs or something. I don't remember what I said in reply, but it couldn't have been smooth. I only recall my main priority being not to pass out, and I achieved it. Chip, on the other hand, couldn't have played it cooler. I forget what he said, too, but his aloofness after such an encounter shook me to the core, and I'd never forget it.

He had no fear. And no conscience.
And I was his favorite target.
This couldn't end well.

T HE GUNPOINT INCIDENT OCCURRED A MERE MONTH INTO
Chip's presence in my life. Jarring as his armed threat may
have been, he was just warming up. Except for a few standout
incidents, the rest of them either blended together in a miserable
soup of memories, or I repressed them altogether.

He pantsed me in the halls twice, including once between
periods when the hallway swarmed with students. I know
Candace Klauss had seen it that time, but she looked away when
I glanced in her direction—I felt like that meant something,
but I wasn't sure what. A teacher had also seen it, which led to a
two-day suspension for Chip. That was the end of the pantsing,
but I wasn't foolish enough to think it marked the end of his
shenanigans.

He'd left me alone, for the most part, until after spring
break. I'd made the mistake of being complacent after so long
without torment, until a glob of chewed-up cafeteria fries arced
its way across the lunchroom and splattered on my face. (As
detestable as this act was, his accuracy was impressive. He'd been
at least fifty feet away.) But the incident that hurt most up to
that point was when he tripped me on the concrete slab of the
bus loading zone—and when I say it hurt, I mean *physically*.
Four-hundred-plus pounds falling flat on an unforgiving surface

like that caused real damage. But no one cared. *Fat guy fall down* is funny. I was convinced I cracked a rib or two, but I never got it checked by a doctor because that would entail telling my parents what'd happened. And that was out of the question.

Somehow, I made it through junior year without getting killed or institutionalized (although there was a stretch after winter break when I strongly considered voluntary admission to the looney bin, just for a reprieve). On the last day of classes, I kept my head on a swivel in anticipation of Chip's last hurrah. For all I knew, he might not be back next year, which would only further diminish his concern for consequences that day. But the coast remained clear. I maintained my vigilance, but the few times I sighted Chip, he didn't even look my way. All was quiet.

I didn't trust it one bit.

Nevertheless, when nature calls, she doesn't leave a message. So as per usual, I answered, and pinched a deuce after eating lunch. My conscious reflection as I dropped the first wave into the toilet was a nagging suspicion as to why Chip hadn't even done his usual pointing at me while I ate, puffing his cheeks and cackling from the other side of the cafeteria. This had become so routine that I only noticed its absence now as I sat on the john.

As it turned out, my thoughts resonated louder than the four thugs milling clandestinely outside my stall. By the time I noticed a shadow moving in the corner of my sight, the stall shook violently in sharp bursts. On the third blast, the door exploded inward, followed by Chip's Timberland boot. The door swung in and smacked my phone out of my hand, stunning me before I had a chance to react. I opened my eyes upon sensing half a dozen or so hands clutching my wrists. Chip and his friends heaved and hoed in unison to rock me off my porcelain seat. Despite leaning my near quarter-ton frame back all I could, they yanked me out of the stall, slamming my face into the corner of the sink counter.

I didn't realize it then, but I must've lost consciousness. There's no other explanation for me opening my eyes and being on my back—I would've remembered turning onto my back. That position is excruciating for me, especially on a flat, hard surface. But beyond this, it takes some time and effort to maneuver my big self in such a way. That entire duration had disappeared.

This missing chunk of time also explains how Chip could have yellow rubber gloves on both hands as he stood over me. The other three assholes stood a safe distance away from him, holding their noses and snickering. I couldn't piece it together, but none of these signs pointed to anything good for Chance Branch.

In unison, two of his henchmen knelt on my arms to pin them down. Chip pressed one knee into my chest and, in one of the gloves, held up what I'd soon learn was one of my very own turds.

"I know you still hungry, fat boy," he said (pronouncing it *bwah*). "Open wide. Here comes the airplane!" He twisted the handful of shit around through the air, making childish propeller sounds as it zoomed in closer to my mouth.

My words were a blur, but they clearly conveyed desperation for mercy. I do remember finishing my plea by shrieking, "*What do you want from me?*" I punctuated this demand for answers by clamping my mouth shut tight.

At this, Chip swung his leg back and then thrust his knee into my groin. Despite the substantial padding around them, his strike crushed my testicles. I blurted that signature *aww* sound associated with a blow to the pills, squeezing my eyes shut and leaving my mouth slightly ajar.

By the time I realized my error, my own lukewarm feces filled my mouth. As horrific as you'd imagine this may have been, I assure you the reality was worse. The taste of it didn't even register amidst all the horror deep in the marrow of my bones. Since I'd been crying, runny snot stuffed my nasal passage, thereby channeling all of my air supply through my mouth—which was now stuffed full of shit. I coughed, sending some of it into my nasal passages, where I'd smell it most intimately.

I know. I still make that same face when I think about it.

And I often do.

Worse yet, my cough had expelled all the air from my lungs. I had no way to breathe unless I cleared the blockage from my mouth.

Taste my own shit, or die—those were my choices. If my tongue didn't find a way to force that dreadful glob out of the way, I'd smother in my own excrement. My options were to accept this fate, or cling to life by savoring the granularity and flavor of my own solid waste, and try to push it out.

I've always imagined my mind being manned by a small army of elite officials. Each of them has a role in every decision I make, every trauma I process, and every lesson I learn. They collaborate in meetings with whiteboards and PowerPoint presentations, determining what's best for the greater Chance, as they see it. They may disagree on this point or the next, but they always reach a consensus via due process. Maybe dry-erase markers get thrown in passion, and maybe one of the guys storms out in exasperation; but in the end, they unify in their solidarity to pursue my best interest. Their system works. After all, there hasn't been a crisis yet that I haven't weathered—and given my lifelong circumstances, that's noteworthy.

In that moment, I could almost see the little guys in my head arguing both courses of action. The most important brain cells sat around a long table in passionate debate. One camp—the more populous one—opposed not only enduring the sensation of pressing my tongue against the fresh turd, but surviving such an event. Any dignity would be unsalvageable, and life would only get worse from there. At least now, if I suffocated, I'd be the victim of an attack, and not the perpetrator of my imminent suicide. Suffocation was the obvious choice.

But the other side of this internal debate was comprised of all the movers and shakers. The big wigs. They stoically retorted that their primary and most essential objective as leaders of this enormous body was survival. So I bit the bullet—or, as it were, the turd—and my tongue pushed it past my teeth and onto the floor with a splat.

Cliché as it might sound, the texture was worse than the taste. And this in no way purports that the taste wasn't wretched. I will never forget that sensation on my tongue, the subtle notes of mostly-digested chicken and broccoli fettuccine alfredo, or the acrid, septic odor that lingered in my nose for days thereafter.

But nothing stuck with me more than the consistency. From that day on, I couldn't eat anything remotely soft or mealy. For me, it was crunchy and dry for life. And nothing gooey with crunchy bits floating around in it, either. Lock me in a room stocked with baked potatoes, overripe fruit, and rocky road ice cream for three months, and you'd find me dead from starvation.

The boisterous laughter and hopping around by my attackers seemed like it happened on the other side of a TV screen. They say when someone endures an overload of pain, they go into a state of shock, and don't even really experience it. Make no mistake, I definitely experienced that incident. But the moments after my tongue pushed the fecal blob onto the floor passed by as if I watched it happen to someone else. Someone I felt really bad for. *Shock* seems like a fitting word for my response.

Against the wishes of every muscle involved in the purging process, remnants of the shitty mush trickled down my throat. Only when the hysterical laughter left the room, and I found myself alone and defeated on the bathroom floor, did I grasp my horrendous reality.

I just ate my shit.

I used my bare hands to wipe what I could off my cheek, and spat out the lingering remains. With a few hard breaths, I psyched myself up for the series of maneuvers necessary to rise to my feet: roll over onto my side, pull my leg up to my chest, get a knee underneath me, grab onto the sink, and stand up. I looked in the mirror, and immediately regretted it. The sight of shit smeared on my face, dribbling down my chin like an infant's meal, repulsed me almost as much as the taste, smell, and mouthfeel.

My own image underneath it disgusted me just as much. Not only was I hideous and gross, I was pathetic. I looked sad, dejected, and weak. Any semblance of dignity I'd ever managed to maintain was now gone. After seventeen years of ignoring daily abuse, I was reduced to this. I didn't know what I'd ever done to deserve it, but clearly I did. Because it happened. And now I had to live my life knowing that.

Maybe I should've chosen death.

I feverishly rinsed my mouth with hand soap and water—doing my best to ignore the chunky bits that broke free from between my teeth. The bitter soap flavor may as well have been ambrosia. I savored the biting antiseptic taste. If there'd been a bottle of bleach handy, I would've swished all its contents in my mouth. I might've even swallowed it.

After that, I went home. I didn't stop at my locker to get my things, I didn't check out at the office, I didn't report this travesty to the principal. I just left.

THE WALK TO MY TRAILER PARK FROM SCHOOL WAS JUST OVER three miles—three times farther than I'd ever traveled on foot at one time in my life. I could've reflected on it as an achievement if I hadn't made the journey entirely on autopilot. In truth, I wasn't even present for that walk. I was sequestered in my own head, searching for the will to continue such a sad existence.

Until then, I'd never considered suicide. But the guys in my head had put the option on the table, and that terrified me.

My parents could rarely be bothered with the tiresome task of showing interest in my day-to-day. The few times they tried, I bored them to yawns with my talk about video games, Hobbits, and graphic novels, so we all stopped pretending those conversations added value for any of us. As I matured, our residential relationship more closely resembled one of roommates than a nuclear family. Unless there were areas of mutual concern, we left each other alone, exchanging cordial smiles in passing.

Dad's role in this partnership primarily centered on finance. If I had a funding need, we'd have a chat about the specifics. As a standing topic of discussion, I attended daily meetings at supper to be reminded how costly my food intake was, and that

I'd better not be drinking his damn beer again. Aside from that, Dad was just sort of . . . *there*—although most of my waking time he wasn't, because he worked third shift at the paper mill. He worked while I slept and slept while I was at school. We'd cross paths in the evening for supper, then go our separate ways in the same room while he watched four hours of cable news before heading off to work. But still, he had a way of being present even when he wasn't in our company.

Mom cooked and cleaned to fulfill her contractual obligations to the Branch household, but the fruits of her labor were always quite elusive. I couldn't confirm it, but I suspected a crack or meth habit kept her busy—meaning most of her active hours were probably dedicated to the unspeakable acts necessary to obtain the money for those drugs. Granted, a lot of this speculation was based on insults hurled at me by Seth and other assholes, but the shoe seemed to fit. She was neurotic and always begged Dad for money, and she was out and about more evenings than she was home. Sometimes I'd be up when she came in late, either breaking down in tears or sitting at the dining room table to count out her cash.

For a brief period of my youth, this gave me crippling anxiety, and I probed for the truth. But after a candid talk with Dad—which falls into my towering pile of repressed memories—I learned to look the other way. If my mom was a crack whore, I didn't need to know. I had enough on my plate (even for someone my size).

But, through all of Mom's turmoil, two things remained constant: supper and laundry. I always had clean clothes, and we always ate together around five, most evenings. Granted, that would be the only formal meal of the day, and our trailer overflowed with a hoard of linens and clothes since Mom often opted for a quick run to Ross or TJ Maxx in favor of an hours-long stint at the laundromat. Impoverished as we may have been, we had more clothes than most affluent households. It may have been a hoarding situation that could earn us a spot on a reality documentary. But in the end, Mom checked all the boxes to earn her keep, so Dad and I rarely protested.

Accordingly, the poo-eating incident raised no flags of concern for them. The last day of school wasn't even marked on their calendars. So, as I trudged through the door—two hours early and red-faced, holding my breath to hide the scent of shit—then meandered past my snoozing dad to my room, Mom rhetorically asked how my day was, never peeling her eyes away from her phone's entrapment.

"Fine," I said.

Fine. Just fiiiiine.

I closed my bedroom door behind me and immediately broke down into hysterical laughter. I stripped off all of my sullied clothes and sprawled onto the floor, giggling uncontrollably until my jugulars strained. While this reaction may seem out of place in hindsight, it felt completely natural in the moment. My body needed to do *something*—or maybe it was my mind that needed it. Crying was unattainable. The sum of my days was but a plentiful series of episodes doing my damnedest *not* to let the world see me weep. It's not as easy as flipping a switch the day I have my own shit shoved in my mouth and *need* to cry.

Laughing, somehow, just felt right. Because when it gets this bad, what else could I do? I bellowed and wheezed, naked on the Berber carpet, until tears streamed from the corners of my eyes and rolled toward the back of my head. Every time the spell seemed ready to wane, I'd replay myself saying *"fine,"* and it would start all over again.

6

THE BREAK BETWEEN JUNIOR AND SENIOR YEAR OFFERED A lot less serenity than I required. It was one of the hottest summers in human history, according to the manic weatherman itching to announce a state of emergency. Existential crisis or not, there was nothing to be taken lightly about being fat and hot in the southern Midwest, especially as a ginger with freckles that grew like bacterial colonies in a petri dish. Matters only worsened in mid-June with the failure of our trailer's air conditioning unit (selfishly mounted in the window of my parents' bedroom). In the middle of day two without Freon, we reduced ourselves to the shameful comfort of a three-foot-deep inflatable Walmart pool, tediously filled into the night by a trickle of tepid well water. After two full days in the Missouri sun, that thirty-five-dollar bright blue vinyl solution for the heat morphed into a grass-killing mosquito incubator that would rest unoccupied until the place itself was destroyed.

Ultimately, the only way to cope was to sweat and hate each other.

I don't think we even made it into July before my parents threatened divorce. Not to say this didn't upset me, but I knew these threats were empty. If not solely due to the legal expense and follow-through required to legitimately absolve a marriage, no way could my folks go through with it. I don't even think they possessed the formal attire necessary to enter a courtroom, let alone the legal know-how to make it happen. Nonetheless, their sentiment wasn't lost on me. I wanted to divorce them, too.

But then the rain came. *Lots* of rain. Weeks of torrential downpours made their mark on our ceiling's Sheetrock—the brown spots sprawling overhead reminding us that the oft-cited *roof over our heads* represented an ongoing expense beyond the provisions of our lot lease. After what seemed like a month, the rains stopped, and the brutal sun used the moisture to boil us all alive.

My life continued to reach new lows, and I wondered where they'd end as I helped my father while he hammered roofing nails into mismatched shingles on top of our trailer. While I could never climb on the roof without destroying it altogether, Dad proposed that as a potential solution—insurance might cover a new roof. I refused on principle, because he'd asked my thoughts on the idea—not out of concern for my safety, but for my opinion on whether it'd work.

Thanks, Pops.

Standing on the side porch all day, exposed to the unobstructed sunlight, I began to take personal offense from the sun. It taunted me. How could it be so high in the sky, and beat down on me so hard, from high noon to 2:30? *Does it move, or not?* No lie, at some points roasting on that porch, I thought about lying face down in that disgusting pool water until I drowned.

About a week before school was to resume, in late August— or, as I think of it, *heat rash season*—I carried out one of my few obligations to the household and did the grocery shopping. I normally dreaded it, but with the air conditioning problem at home, I looked forward to the cool environment. Obviously, I'd prefer to trade places with Mom, and sit in the car with the A/C blasting, but that role was reserved for taxpayers. Regardless, I'd make the most of my opportunities and linger in the produce and freezer sections. This time, as I feigned interest in asparagus and brussels sprouts for a solid ten minutes, my world changed forever.

"Excuse me," a sweet, feminine voice said. I whipped my head around to behold a dirty blonde with a dark tan, wearing a top tied in a knot above her midriff and denim shorts so short the pockets peeked out from underneath. "Do you know where they keep the papayas?"

I tried to formulate a response other than *no*, despite not knowing what a papaya even looked like. (That's one of those fruits I still don't believe anyone actually eats.) I caressed my chin while scanning the produce section for clues. "Umm, I'm afraid I don't," I finally said, my disappointment sincere.

"Ah, ok." She flapped a piece of paper in her hand. "I'm gonna have a heck of a time getting everything on this list. I'm new in town, so this place is like another planet compared to the Piggly Wiggly." She flashed a coquettish smile.

Her southern drawl mesmerized me. The way she said *Piggly Wiggly* made me want to put her in my pocket and take her home. Her face struck me—not just in its beauty, but its unique features. The plumpness of her nose and her slanted forehead just looked right on her. But her eyebrows—they were *perfect*. And not like the ones some girls have, that looked like they were drawn on with a Sharpie. No, these gems were a product of excellent genes.

It almost felt like I'd met her before. No doubt, she was way too hot for me. But then again, *any* girl was. I knew any display of interest was futile—but no matter how unattractive I may be, my overactive teenage testicles hijacked the controls of my mind in situations like this. They didn't pass on any opportunities.

"Well, maybe I can help you out with some of the other stuff on there," I said, gesturing at the paper. This was true—I'd come to know this store's layout well over the years and could find almost anything. Just not papayas and other hoity-toity non-necessities.

She handed me the list. "I'm Trinity, by the way."

Trinity. Such a pretty name. Though I tried my best not to get too attached, a part of my brain immediately pondered where on my body a *Trinity* tattoo would look best. "I'm Chance," I said.

Trinity cupped her ear and leaned closer. "Come again?"

"Chance."

"*Trance?*"

"*Chance.* As in, you know—like, *take a chance.*"

"Ohh, *Chance.* I like that name! Nice to meet you. And I sure do appreciate your help."

I told her it was my pleasure, and it most certainly was. We meandered through the store, making small talk as I led her to each item on the list. I learned she was a cheerleader with aspirations to make the squad at Mizzou—the casual name for the University of Missouri. She hated store-brand products, loved licorice, and always needed help getting items off the top shelves. Apparently, she'd had a hard time making friends, which I told her I could relate to pretty well. Her family had just relocated to Chandler's Marsh from Mississippi for her dad's work. As we picked up the last item on her list, and I ignored my phone vibrating in my pocket, we stopped our walk together to part ways.

"Are you a football player?" she said. "You sure are built like one."

I shook my head as slowly as I could, trying not to let my extra chins jiggle. My voice came out a mournful, masculine burr. "Nah, not anymore. Injured my ankle last season."

"Aw, that's too bad. My uncle's a scout for Ole Miss (the University of Mississippi). He'd want me to scoop you up in a heartbeat if you were still playing."

After maintaining my discipline throughout this exchange, my mouth finally fell open. It *had* to be a sign. What were the odds of this? I reconsidered my hatred for exercise at the off chance of being scouted by a collegiate program, and impressing this tender morsel before me. "Is that a fact?"

"On my mother's life," she said, raising a hand. She pulled a pen from her purse and snatched the list from my hand. "Tell you what. Here's my number. Why don't you give me a call sometime and we can talk more about it? You got around just fine in this store. I gotta believe you can do the same in cleats." She handed me the paper with a smile.

After a goodbye I don't quite remember because I was hyper-focused on remaining upright, I turned down a random aisle and studied her handwriting. It was so bubbly and feminine that pure instinct compelled me to sniff the paper in case it smelled like her potent, sweet perfume. I heard a stifled laugh behind me, but turned around to find no one other than an old man. *Screw you, boomer*, I thought, then stared him down as I sniffed it again.

Needless to say, female attention like this was a first. I wondered what powers might be at play to make something like this happen. What were the odds Trinity would move to this town *and* be related to a college football scout? And on top of that, what made her approach *me*, of all people, for help with her grocery list? As much as I tried to temper my optimism, it was hard not to entertain the possibility that this beautiful girl might actually see something in me she liked.

I bellowed a laugh at the next thought that ran through my head.

Yeah, right, I thought. *Fat chance!*

My vibrating phone finally got my attention, so I answered it. Mom was appalled that I hadn't gotten anything on our own list yet, all because—as I put it—I'd been chatting with a friend I ran into. I wasn't sure whether her skepticism stemmed from the claim that I'd talked with someone for so long, or that I actually had a friend to do it with, but I didn't care. My preoccupied mind took its sweet time running through the grocery list as I tried to hide my involuntary grin from passing strangers.

Of course, I had to play it cool. I may not have been fighting the ladies off with a stick, but I knew how to dance the dance. I didn't call Trinity that evening—although I strongly considered sending her a text. Instead, all I did that night was lie awake, staring at the ceiling as I flexed my pecs and abs in a passive attempt to trim whatever I could from my physique before I saw Trinity again.

I felt myself being taken prey by a ruthless predator called *hope*. I tried in vain not to become mesmerized, citing my own formed belief that hope is for the fortunate. For people like me, it was a devastating drug. A narcotic, or hallucinogen, serving no other purpose than to twist a less merciful reality into something palatable.

7

BY DAYBREAK, I WAS STILL AT IT. I GAVE UP ON SLEEP AND LET my aching muscles relax from the convulsion exercises. My fantasies had wandered so far that Trinity and I stood at the altar before a packed congregation of Ole Miss Alumni and fans. I'd get selected high in the NFL draft, but I'd remain true to her for seeing my value long before my impending stardom. I went ahead and worked this into my vows. The Missouri sun forced me out of my bed before I started sweating through the sheets.

Mom was quite surprised—concerned, even—that I'd arisen without an alarm or rap on the door. Her suspicion only sharpened when I failed to finish breakfast. I told her it was too hot to eat, quelling her fears with an easy smile. In fact, I had to fight to keep that silly grin from sneaking onto my face as I continued daydreaming.

By noon, my nervous energy peaked to the point I started to worry myself. I'd walked half a mile to a nearby creek and fished with pieces of a worm that took me an hour to dig up as bait, using a neglected fishing rod (I use the term *neglected,* but I think that rod had been under our trailer since before we bought it). None of this behavior fit my norm, and I still felt inclined to do more. Sweaty, sleepless, and starving, I strongly considered trying to make the trek home solely with lunges to work off a bit more weight.

A desperate voice deep in my head—probably one of those high-ranking guys bent on my survival—screamed in dissent, so I took my shoes off and cooled my feet in the running creek instead. Once my heart rate came down and my body cooled, I hit a wall. The possibility that I might not have the energy to make it home became very real. If I did make it, odds were that I'd sleep for an entire day. And if that happened, it would make two full days I didn't call Trinity, which wouldn't be okay. Waiting one day showed proper restraint. Two days or more would be reckless hubris. As my window of opportunity closed, I pulled out my cell phone and prepared to call her. (Of course, within an hour of getting home from the store, I'd already added her as a contact, and designated her Instagram profile picture as her photo.)

I took the deepest breath of my life and hit *call*. After five rings, she answered. Even the way she said *hello* with a southern accent made my heart bang against my sternum.

"Hey, Trinity! *Chance* here," I said, enunciating so hard my face muscles strained.

"Oh, hey! How are ya, hon?"

Hon! She called me *hon*. I smiled so wide she might've heard it. I chose my words as I'd conditioned myself to—avoiding *S*, *th-*, and *ch-* sounds like land mines. "Good, I'm good. How about you?"

Just as I thought *so far, so good*, there was a pause. I checked my screen to ensure we hadn't gotten disconnected. Just before I said "hello?" to check this, she answered as though the delay had never happened.

"Oh, me? I'm good. Just trying to stay out of this heat, ya know? Jeez Louise! I don't even think it got this hot back in

Mississippi (pronounced *Miss-sippy* in her charming dialect)."

We spent a good two or three minutes talking about the heat, which was all but customary under these inhumane conditions. I made her laugh a couple of times with quips about the effect of heat like this on someone my size. Her giggle made me lie back against the rough bank of the creek and admire the canopy overhead. Her laugh meant me no harm, and I don't think I grasped the rarity of this sensation until that moment. I closed my eyes, squeezing the happy tears out, before recapturing my casual tone.

"Anyway, you got me thinking about football again. Have you talked to your uncle about me at all?"

Again, a stint of silence prompted me to check the connection before she answered. "You know, I haven't—I sent him a message just to say hi, but he hasn't said anything back yet. He's a pretty busy guy, as you can imagine. Training camp and all that."

"Right, right." I slapped my forehead. Some football player I was, oblivious to football season starting less than a month away.

"But I'll tell ya what," she said. "It'll sure get his attention if he could see the size of you. Would you be interested in coming to my place for a little photo shoot? Nothing too serious, just a couple shots to send him. If he could see you standing next to me, I'm sure he'll be here in time to meet you at the front door on your way out."

The thought of standing close to her made me feel as if I were floating away. The scent of her syrupy perfume returned to my nose. I imagined making my move, taking her tiny shoulder in my big hand as we faced the camera, and squeezing her against my side. The remainder of our conversation dissipated in a fog of exhilaration, exhaustion, and disbelief, but I retained enough lucidity to agree on a time for this rendezvous—tomorrow night. She'd let me know when she was through with supper so I could head over. I hung up, and immediately thereafter she texted me her address.

I lay there, my ass now partially immersed in the creek's rapids, convincing myself I wasn't dreaming. My suspicions had validity because none of what had occurred since being in bed felt like reality. I don't wake up early. I don't leave food on the plate. I don't dig for worms, fish, or venture a half mile from home on foot without a destination—or even *with* one. And I sure as shit don't talk to pretty girls on the phone, or make them laugh, or agree to meet them in person. Only the torturous heat, searing pain in my tailbone, and numbness in my legs reminded me that this was indeed reality. I got to my feet and began the journey home.

I staggered along the roadside in my effort to multitask, looking up Trinity's address on Google Maps. I zoomed in on her duplex, tried to memorize the route there, and studied the cars in the driveway—even though they probably weren't hers since her family had just moved in. It still told me something to know what kind of cars the previous tenants owned. What, exactly, I couldn't say—but I wasn't about to leave anything a mystery.

The next twenty-four hours went by almost instantly. After a shower, I slept from 3 p.m. that day until just before noon the next. Don't get me wrong, I love sleeping. But I can say with certainty that I'd never before slept for twenty-one continuous hours. I might've slept even longer if Mom hadn't awoken me with several firm slaps on the cheek. I opened my eyes to see her holding a mirror under my nose.

"Jesus, Ma," I said, swatting the mirror away. "I'm alive!"

"Well, you sleep like the dead, Chance. 'Scuse me for caring."

I gestured at the mirror in her hand. "Why the hell'd you slap me if you can see I'm breathing?"

"Because you *weren't* breathing," she said. "Mirror didn't fog up at all! I shook your arm to make sure you hadn't gone stiff, too, but you didn't even budge. I thought you were gone! Bout gave me a heart attack, boy!"

I will forever look back on this exchange as the first warning of the severity of my sleep apnea. It's quite possible that without that sleepless night, followed by that wakeless day scaring the piss out of my mom, I never would've gotten it checked out. As it went, the doctor told us without intervention, the apnea might very well cause a heart event, even death, without warning. It wouldn't be long before I started sleeping with a lifesaving medical monstrosity called a CPAP machine.

Therefore, it's plausible to say that by this chain of events alone, meeting Trinity saved my life.

After supper, I asked Mom to give me a haircut before she went *out with the girls*, as she put it (never once did I meet any of these supposed girls, nor could she tell me anything about them). She committed to giving me a "quick trim" due to her time constraints.

Before I assign her too much blame for what happened next, I should cop to my own share.

I've known this woman all my life, which is plenty long enough to recognize the warning signs of this being a bad idea. First, she had obvious tremors. Maybe it was drug or alcohol withdrawals, maybe not—either way, any cogent mind could see that those hands had no business holding cutting implements. Secondly, Mom never does anything well if she's rushed. Tell her to butter a slice of toast, no problem. Tell her to do it in ten seconds, and she's liable to turn that toast into bread crumbs, then run off in a tizzy. But lastly—and most egregiously—I persisted in asking the favor when her first answer was no. I may succeed in persuading my mom to submit to my demands, but her final act of resistance will always be to ensure I regret doing so.

And that I did.

I certainly didn't see the incident through such an objective lens upon seeing her handiwork. What I'd asked for was the same haircut she'd always given me—a scissoring of all my tightly curled locks to about the width of her finger, with a graduated fade with the clippers along the sides and back. Over the years, she'd perfected this (barring any of the aforementioned poor conditions). What she bargained for instead was a *trim*, which we both understood to be just the fade portion of the cut. "Just get the shag off my ears and neck," as I'd often phrased it. This would've been an adequate result.

What I got, however, was nothing short of an assault. The "fade" was a scalp-tight shave ending abruptly at the crown, accentuating the puffiness of my curly, copper afro. I looked like a redheaded mushroom.

Mom ignored my tirade as she threw the barbering tools in their case, zipped it shut, and gathered her things to head out the door. Dad normally would've admonished me for the way I spoke to Mom as she left, but this time he was too busy laughing at me. There was a moment he gathered himself enough to take a stern tone, but he lost his composure when I turned to face him. I'm sure it was hilarious, given how seldom my father laughed like that, but the humor couldn't have been more lost on me.

"Ma, are you seriously leaving right now? Look at my friggin' head!"

She rifled through her purse for her car keys. "I know, hon—it ain't my best work. But the damage is done. I'm surely not skilled enough to fix it. After all, they make barbers get thousands of hours of experience. And now you see why."

I looked at the ceiling and tugged on my remaining hair. "What am I supposed to do now? I look like a damn fool!"

"Oh, go on now—it ain't *that* bad. Just put a ball cap on and no one'll be the wiser. I gotta go now, hon. Sorry I did such a bad job. You know how I get when I'm hurried."

What could I say back? I *did* know. And she was right—the damage was done. If anyone on earth could fix my hair, she'd be at the bottom of that list of billions. I'd be better off shaving my head. It might even make the locals respect me a bit more.

Trinity still hadn't texted or called, so I went ahead with my post-haircut shower. If anything could make this butchering look worse, it was water. The squiggly line circumventing my head only came through clearer in the absence of hair clippings. I grabbed my phone and told Trinity that tonight might not be the best and asked if we could do another night instead.

While I awaited her text reply, I decided I might be able to fix Mom's disaster. Without consideration for the possibility that—despite my verbal assertion to the contrary—I *could* make it worse, I plugged the clippers in and went to work. The result resembled a puffy mohawk, with random chunks gashed out from the back. (At my size, reaching behind to cut the back of my head is a great enough challenge without having to do so one-handed, using two mirrors.) Only one thing could exacerbate this situation.

My phone sounded the bottle cap notification I'd designated to texts from Trinity. I stared at her response with dread.

> Aww, hon. It has to be tonight if we're doing this. My photographer friend is already here

Photographer? I thought. *What happened to "nothing too serious?"*

This left me with two choices—both of which burned a hole in my stomach. Either I'd cancel and fracture our budding trust, or I'd show up looking like literally the biggest idiot she'd ever seen in her life. I paced the small floor of my room as I clawed my preposterous hair, racking my brain to produce a third option, when she sent another message telling me to head on over. The winking kissy-face emoji with which she punctuated this message would've stalled my heartbeat under any circumstances, but now it threatened to stop my pulse for good.

I concealed my mangled mop with a Kansas City Royals ball cap. After a long sigh, I responded, telling her I'd be right over. The transmission of that text bounced off the nearest cell tower and rerouted toward Trinity's phone before I froze. I hadn't thought out this phase of the operation. My mom had left with one of our two vehicles. My dad had to be at work in less than three hours, but he'd have to give me a ride.

While that may not seem disastrous on the surface, I covered my face with both hands because I knew better. Because I knew Dad.

As I mentioned, Dad stayed out of my business. Like, to a fault. But that's true in part because I made an effort not to get him involved—we all did. You see, once Dad gets pestered with someone else's problem, he takes full ownership of it. Soup to nuts, he was going to get all the information, make a categorical assessment of the problem, formulate a solution, and implement it—anyone else was but a spectator to behold his magical touch. I'd bet my kingdom he was the same way at work, which would explain his supervisory position . . . and lack of work friends.

So I knew it wouldn't be as simple as asking for a ride. I'd be submitting to an interrogation, and thereby relinquish any agency I had in this tenuous affair with Trinity. I wasted a good five minutes installing and trying to use the Uber app before realizing there was no way to use it without a bank account or some other digital form of money. I didn't have money in *any* form, but it'd be way easier—albeit not easy—to ask Dad for a twenty-dollar bill than the alternative, which remained my only recourse.

"Hey, Pops," I said, leaning on the doorjamb. "Any chance you could drop me at a friend's house real quick?"

He lowered the TV volume from deafening to almost

tolerable. "*What* friend?"

"Over on Peacock Road. It's too far to walk, and Mom took her car." (Note my lack of pronoun usage, and subsequent pivot. Not my first rodeo.)

Dad muted the TV and scowled at me for an awkward duration. It looked mean, but I knew this was just his thinking face. "Yeah, but *who?* You don't have any friends, do ya? Least, none I know of."

This was the moment of truth—literally. The point during Dad's examination when I had to decide whether honesty would carve a shorter or easier path to the desired outcome than a lie. If deception looked to be the better option, I'd better have my details in order. The latter could only be a viable choice with adequate premeditation, which did not fit this scenario. So, honesty it was.

"It's a new friend."

He tumbled his hand. "Gimme a name."

"Trinity."

"*Trinity?* 'Zat a girl's name?"

"Yep."

At this, his contemplative frown softened into a rotten-toothed smile. I thought he was about to laugh at me, but instead, he smirked. "You don't say! Is she fat like you, I hope? Otherwise, I hope you'd wonder what she wants with ya."

"I'm sure she'd like to lose a few pounds." (Neither truth nor lie, but probably true. The way I understood it, all girls wanted to lose weight.)

He chuckled. "Don't be making any fat babies, now. You got protection?"

I rolled my eyes. "C'mon now, Pops."

"You got a ride back? I gotta get ready and go to work soon.

I ain't your taxi service."

"I can get a ride home." (Not true *yet*, but I'd figure something out.)

He sucked his teeth and offset his jaw—promising signs his questions ran thin. "Then how come you can't get a ride there, too?"

"I don't wanna ask her to drive all the way here, then back to her place, then do it again when it's time to leave. But I guess that's what I'll do, if you won't drive me." (Man, I'd gotten good at this.)

He stared at the corner of the room, as though he expected a cockroach to stand up and tell him to think again. "Better get your shoes on. Takes ya twenty damn minutes to."

Bam! I needed a win, and I got it. Sure, my hair was jacked, and I had no exit strategy, but maybe this small victory would give me some momentum. And now that my dad knew the truth (mostly), I could openly prepare and express my nerves. I brushed my teeth with extra toothpaste, showered myself in Axe body spray, and wore the one nice shirt I owned—a white, collared button-up. I strapped my best pair of Adidas onto my feet (which only took five minutes, by the way) and checked myself over one last time.

It's funny how confidence changes what's in the mirror. The reflection in that same bedroom mirror so often showed me a pathetic young man—at times when I *didn't* have butchered hair. But now, at the mere prospect of being desired, I stood straighter. I looked myself in the eye. I lifted my chin. I was Instagram ready. Dad's hollering broke me away from this rare episode of self-admiration.

Once we got in his truck, I realized it meant phase two of the interrogation. Granted, few ways existed for me to lose the ride

I'd won in the first phase, but it still posed a risk. Considering all the uncertainty running through my own mind, keeping Dad at arm's length became imperative. I didn't need him planting seeds of doubt in my head, or throwing off my delicate mojo. I gave him the address, and he keyed it into his navigation app.

"Looks like she's slumming it, huh?" he said with a snort. "Them duplexes ain't cheap, especially in a seller's market, like it is. Do you know if her family bought or rents?"

I decided the best defense would be a good offense. "Come on, Pops. You think that's the kind of thing kids my age talk about?"

"Can't hurt to ask."

I wasn't sure if he meant his question to me, or if he was urging me to broach the topic with Trinity. Either way, the old man's lack of touch made me snicker. Apparently, this was an egregious affront, because Dad half-turned to leer at me, then shifted in his seat. He wiped the corners of his mouth.

Whenever he did that, a lecture inevitably followed.

"I'm not clueless about how to talk to girls, ya know," he said, keeping his eyes on the road. "Your mother ain't my first, not by a long stretch. Matter of fact, I took two different girls to two different junior proms. I did a hell of a lot better than *you* ever will. I ain't even heard you mention your prom, and you're heading into senior year now, ain't ya?"

"I never said you were clueless, Pops."

My response meant nothing. His steadfast sermon continued like a laden freight train as we turned down Peacock Road. "I bet I'd *still* have 'em lined up at my door if your mama didn't tie me down by getting knocked up with you. I tell ya . . . lot of days I wonder what might've been. She ain't touched me in *months*, and I coulda had *anyone* before our shotgun wedding.

Know what I mean?"

I nodded, glassy eyes forward.

This part of the road was straight, so he held his stare on me for a few seconds before facing ahead again. I welcomed the awkward silence until he broke it with a question that hit me like a strong left hook. "Be honest. You ever wonder if you're mine?"

My head snapped to face him, but he kept his eyes forward now. I said the only thing my oversized tongue could manage. "*What?*"

"I know *I* do. Ain't a day that goes by with you waddling by, shaking the whole damn trailer, that I don't wonder if your mama cheated on me with some fat bastard." Now he met my eyes. "Look at my scrawny ass. Think about the genetics and all that *sciency* shit. Pundit squares or whatever. You really think you came outta my dick? Cause I sure as hell don't."

Bam. Just like that, mojo *gone*. And not a moment too soon, either. As we pulled up behind the three cars in Trinity's driveway, I unlatched the seat belt. "Thanks for the talk, Pops. Have a good night at work."

I slammed the door in the middle of him saying something, but I didn't hear or care what. Nothing Dad said to me ever really mattered more than I let it, but this time he'd hit me where it hurt, and at the worst possible time. While his words hurt, what cut me to the core of my soul was the cruel casualness of his tone. *Hey kiddo, I don't think you're my son. I never have. Oh, hey, don't forget breath mints!*

In my rage, I failed to avoid the ass end of the red Pontiac Sunfire parked closest to the house, and rocked it on its chassis. I refused to look back and give Dad the satisfaction of seeing my face, but I was almost certain I'd left a dent in the little car's rear quarter panel.

I rang the doorbell and waited to hear the old man's truck back out, but it idled in the driveway until the front door opened. A normal kid might assume his dad wanted to make sure he got in okay. But me? I knew he lurked only to catch a glimpse of Trinity.

10

Trinity greeted me with a warm smile and invited me in. Her eyes were glassy, and she smelled like a skunk, but she still looked like a goddess. She wore an Ole Miss sweatshirt that covered whatever she wore as bottoms—if she even had any on—and sickeningly adorable bunny slippers on her feet. Her air conditioning was frigidly divine, making the heft of the conversation with my father—or whatever he was—evaporate like the beads of sweat on the back of my neck. The living room was undecorated, which made sense, given how long she'd lived there. I couldn't help but notice a cluster of pictures hung on the wall, with an obvious void in the middle, as though one had been removed. An end table also had framed photos, but one of them lay on its face. Clearly, her home life had some complications beyond what she'd disclosed to me—but who was I to judge after what I'd just learned of my own home life?

A familiar face emerged from the kitchen, a camera hanging around his neck. I couldn't place his name, but I definitely knew his face. I squinted at him just as Trinity introduced him.

"This is my photographer friend, Todd," she said with a presenting hand.

I pointed at him in recognition. "Todd Simpson, right?" I phrased it as a question, but I had no doubt. He'd come to the school recently, maybe sophomore year. He played cornerback on the football team. But there was some other reason his face struck me.

He nodded. His reticence eradicated any nagging suspicion I had that his presence posed a threat to me and my intentions, but I still itched for his departure. I wanted the photo shoot portion of this visit to be done, so I could advance my agenda with Trinity—whatever that might exactly be.

She offered me sweet tea, with the contingency that it'd come as sugary as they make it back in Miss-sippy, which I politely declined in favor of a glass of water. I cited the heat and already surpassing my recommended daily sugar allowance (which, surprisingly, was a lie).

As she and Todd disappeared into the kitchen to get my ice water, I took a seat on the couch. I settled in place just in time to rise again at the emergence of a bearded butterball with a greying crew cut, wearing a wifebeater top that'd likely lived up to its crude name. He toddled into the room with a can of Milwaukee's Best in his fist, slowing his pace at the sight of me. As he neared, he had to look up to meet my gaze.

"My lord in heaven," he said, tonguing the fat plug of dip in his lower lip. "I dunno who you are, but please tell me you play for the Spartans." Even the scalp beneath his short hair had a reddish tan.

"Not anymore, sir," I said with a mournful shake of my head. I pointed at my leg. "Ankle injury."

He glanced at my foot, then his unfocused eyes tried to reset onto mine. "And? You rehabbing it or what?"

I nodded too hard. "Of course, of course. Always." I extended my hand with uncharacteristic assurance. "My name's Chance. Chance Branch."

He wheezed a laugh and slapped my hand away sloppily. "Oh, 'zat right? Well there, *Shantsbrandt*, I'm Trinity's daddy (pronounced *deddy*). But you can call me Mister Smith, if your folks raised ya right." The free hand on his belly pressed out a long, reverberating belch. "Or Roscoe, if they didn't." He plopped hard onto the couch and spat into a half-filled Mountain Dew bottle on the end table.

"Oh, okay," I said. "So, um—Mr. Smith—is it your brother or her mother's who's the scout for Ole Miss?"

Trinity reappeared from the kitchen and rushed to grab my arm. "Daddy, please don't pester my friends like that, will you not? Great day! Chance, come on with me. I'm so sorry about my daddy. He's drunk as a shithouse skunk."

With my red Solo cup of ice water in her free hand, she dragged me up the stairs, but I turned back just in time to glimpse her dad's confused frown as he nestled into a limp posture on the couch. At the top of the stairs, I peeked into a vacant bedroom and spied a large gun safe—*nothing unusual*, I thought. As she led me down a short hallway, a cacophony of alarms sounded in my mind.

But I made the willful choice to ignore them.

She pulled me into the dark glow of a bedroom and shut the door behind us. It reeked of freshly smoked weed, and every wall shimmered with iridescent black light posters. Weird techno music played softly under the ambient whirr of an air purifier. My white shirt gleamed like a light all its own under the ambient ultraviolet—and as I looked down at it, I came to the stark realization that the mustard stain had not, in fact, come out (at least, I *hoped* it was mustard). Just as I crossed my arms to conceal it, Trinity pushed me into a sitting position on the bed. She sat cross-legged next to me and handed me the red cup.

I stared at her greenish-glowing teeth as Todd entered the room and sat in the swivel desk chair, the old-school digital camera still dangling from his neck.

"So, Chance," she said with a giggle. "I figured we could loosen up a bit before we got to taking pictures and all that." Todd relit a half-smoked joint, handed it to her, and she puffed on it. "You do get high, right?"

I wasn't sure why she thought this a safe assumption, but it wasn't. Sure, I *had* gotten high before, but I didn't make a habit of it. Pot had a tendency to make me paranoid, which for me makes for a debilitating side effect when everyone *really is* staring at you at all times. But rather than try to explain this, I caved to peer pressure like a poorly portrayed character in a low-budget PSA.

"Pssh. *Of course*," I said.

She flashed her eyebrows. "Want me to blow you a shotgun?"

I responded in the affirmative, but I don't recall forming any actual words. I was too stymied by this implication to conjure a coherent verbal answer. Whatever I did elicited another delightful titter from Trinity.

You see, blowing a shotgun had two possible meanings—at least that I was aware of. One meant that she would place the burning end of the joint in her mouth, put the other end close to mine, and she'd blow raw smoke for me to inhale. The other, much more intimate meaning was that she'd inhale the joint like normal, then lock lips with me to transfer her lungful of smoke directly to my airway. Either way, her pretty face would be very close to mine, placing me in a very new and terrifying position—but also a very tantalizing one.

If we touch lips, will it count as my first kiss? I wondered.

To be clear—and perhaps state the obvious—I'd always

assumed my first kiss would never organically occur. I accepted early in adolescence that this rite of passage would come late in life, if ever, and the circumstances would be nothing to brag about. Either I'd mine the social landscape for a woman as intoxicated and unattractive as myself, or I'd have to outright pay some lady of the night to check that box (and a few others) off my bucket list.

The only possible exception to this perpetual resignation was Candace Klauss. But in truth, before this very evening, I hadn't entertained the possibility of a romantic, voluntary kiss any more than I'd considered the terms of my final will and testament. So, under the current circumstances, I was just about as unprepared as I could be. I needed a moment to deliberate all this, and I bought myself that invaluable chunk of time by holding up a finger and chugging half my supply of ice water.

Before I looked up from setting the cup down, Trinity straddled my lap and took a long pull from the joint. My heart thumped as the realization set in that she was seconds away from planting her glossy lips onto mine. There was a moment of whooshing in my ears, and I wondered if this might kill me. I could die of a coronary right there on her bed—and if I did, I'd stand before St. Peter without regret. Trinity choked back a cough, then leaned in, closing her gorgeous sapphire eyes.

I'd heard the term *out-of-body experience* before, and I always pictured my ethereal spirit hovering above my fat body—the lifeless vehicle I equated with my sense of self. But in the instant Trinity's soft lips enchanted mine, that term took on a different meaning. Something happened inside me, and I was no longer trapped inside my cumbersome, frumpy form—because that wasn't me. It couldn't be. By whatever miracle the universe bestowed upon me, I felt what it was like to be someone else.

Someone normal. Someone accepted.

To be desired.

I wasn't just Fat Chance. My soul had ejected from that bulky body and somehow landed in the cockpit of a vehicle worthy of this beautiful girl's touch. Shivers rattled my spine as she wrapped her dainty fingers around the back of my neck and kept my mouth engaged with hers, breathing unimaginable life into me in the form of secondhand weed smoke.

As enthralling as this communion was, it *hurt*. Literally. Immediately, my body registered the data and indicated to me that the gasses I'd received were noxious—mostly carbon dioxide and poison smoke—and, most importantly, contained *zero* oxygen. My chest heaved like a supernova in the milliseconds before its fatal burst. I tried with all the willpower in my being to avoid it, but my body exercised its veto authority and expelled the toxic breath outward with great force, sending with it a stringy mass of saliva and phlegm.

I opened my eyes to Trinity grimacing with one eye shut, sealed by a gooey glob propelled from my own passages. Her lips compressed with the force of every muscle in her face to seal out the strand of goo waiting to breach any opening. She shuddered, her expression frozen as if any hint of movement would only make the moment more real. After a second, she flapped her hands frantically and screamed through her nose in a signal for whatever help might be available.

Even where I sat, it felt like a sick movie. Time moved in funny ways, and facts hit me in sporadic waves. No way was this happening. Just . . . *no way*. I did *not* just hock a giant loogie onto the prettiest face that'd ever shown me regard, let alone the only one to ever kiss me. Detachment from this reality was my only choice until I had proof positive that it was not some sort of delusion. Soon, I'd wake up or snap out of my catatonic state in a padded room, and reconnect with actual reality, however grim it might be.

Anything but this.

Todd's sputtering laugh and drones of "Oh my God" were the first clues I wasn't dreaming. The truth hit me like a bucket of ice when Trinity snatched a shirt from him and ran from the room, whimpering in disgust.

The black light, weird music, and creeping influence of marijuana did not help clarify my delirium. Todd's snickering as he tapped his phone screen, completely ignoring my presence or predicament, only reinforced my hope that this entire night might fade from existence. I'd wake up in my undersized bed, in my sweltering double-wide home—fat, sad, and alone like always, and none of this would've happened. It'd be a nightmare I'd keep to myself until my dying day.

Please, God.

Either from abject horror or the weed, my mouth had gone dry, so I reached for the Solo cup on the nightstand. My arms always felt heavy—because they were—but now it felt like I wore weighted sleeves. I managed to grab the cup and down the rest of the cold water before collapsing back into a contorted heap on the twin bed. As I tried to fix my eyes at a point on the ceiling, the darkly-glowing room around me began to swirl, ratcheting after a quarter-spin, and then repeating. The last thing I remember from that night was Trinity's face looking down at me, devoid of any makeup or emotion as she toweled it off. I couldn't make out her words, but her tone rang clinical in whatever she said to Todd—and to whomever else was in the room—before my eyelids sealed me off from the scene.

I AWOKE TO DAYLIGHT, WHICH JARRED ME TO SIT UP FASTER than I could ever recall doing before. Surely, my parents wondered about my whereabouts, and perhaps they'd even called the cops. I reached for my right-front pocket to retrieve my cell phone when I realized I was stark naked. Sitting atop the twin bed, I looked around, trying to answer a litany of questions with competing priority.

Where are my clothes? Why am I nude? Where's my phone? Where's Trinity? Did she see me naked? Where's Todd, with his goddamn camera? Did he use it . . . while I was naked? What time is it? What happened last night? How did I pass out so suddenly? What's my next move?

The first of these questions to be answered was the location of my clothes. Be it a curse or a blessing, I easily identified my giant pants among the mound of laundry in the corner of the room. As I put them on, I caught sight of something on my chest. Dark markings circled my nipples, but I couldn't discern what the pattern was supposed to be. I looked for a mirror as I wondered whether the graffiti on my body was the kind made in good fun because I'd fallen asleep too soon, or the hurtful kind I strongly suspected. I put the pants on, as well as the crinkled shirt beneath them, without fastening the buttons.

As I stepped out into the hallway, the house felt vacant. The stillness broke with the emergence of two orange tabby cats who trotted gleefully to rub against my ankles. I located the bathroom and went in, taking a deep breath to behold whatever the mirror showed when I flicked on the lights.

First, and not entirely horrific, I noticed that my eyebrows had been darkened with permanent marker and shaped into an angry expression. No biggie. A devilish goatee had also been scrawled onto my chin, which actually made me chuckle. On my right cheek, a sophomoric drawing of a penis pointed at the corner of my lips. I then pulled my shirt open, revealing the *coup de grâce*.

All I could do was stare.

Cartoonish lines framed my nipples, making them look like cross-eyed pink pupils. A crooked pair of lines formed the shape of a nose down my sternum, all the way to my navel. A bushy mustache had been drawn above my belly button, and waxy red lips traced around it, giving the appearance that my torso was a cross-eyed, whistling, mustached buffoon.

The betrayal hadn't set in yet. My first reaction was to laugh. Objectively, this act of vandalism looked silly, and it made me chuckle. Then I decided to undo my pants and check below the waist.

My ears throbbed as I absorbed what I saw. I lifted the shameful flap of blubber I loathsomely referred to as my *pooch*, revealing a set of markings on my leg next to my genitals. They were hash marks about a half inch apart, and each was labeled with some mocking measurement of my manhood. The first was marked as "flea dick." The next was "squirrel cock." I made a conscious effort not to read the next three hash labels, inferring their ruthless theme without making myself ingest it. Capping this off was the sad face drawn on the tip of my penis.

The full gravity of this humiliation wouldn't set in for quite some time, but a potent cocktail of preliminary truths hit me right away.

My body, however grotesque it might be to anyone but me, had been defiled.

This was a crime.

After all the abuse I'd endured in my then seventeen years, I'd grown accustomed to a lot of emotional and psychological anguish. I'd been a target for all assholes of Planet Earth, ages three and up. I'd weathered the endless advice as to how I could lead a normal life and avoid being lazy and shameless—easy, just get up and go! Stop being a fatass, and be a responsible person who exercises and eats rabbit food! Grains, lean legumes, and nothing more, you oaf! I'd heard every insult lurking in the bowels of the bottomless stockpiles of slurs set aside for people like me, to the point that the assaults stopped hurting.

Think about that. Imagine the world hating your body so much, so often, and with such pointed fervor that it doesn't even bother you anymore. You can't.

But that was the only world I knew.

Being as big and undesirable as I've always been is like building a tolerance to getting slashed by razor blades on every square inch of my body, day in and day out, every day of my life, and still being called weak by people with bodies approved by the human race. It hurts, but you unfortunately get used to it.

Your size is your soul. Your weight is the inverse of your worth. Who cares who you are, what you feel, or what you have to offer to society? Who cares how smart you are, how kind you can be, or what your soul is made of? You're *fat*. The lowest caste of human existence. Absolute trash, condemned by the hasty glances of billions of perfect strangers.

Every day. Forever.

Can you imagine that?

Then, pretend that one day, those routine razor blades transform into swords. The torture was always relentless, but you'd found a way to cope. To survive it. Now the cuts run deep enough to kill you. To drain you of your life force. Gashing you like cleavers through slaughtered livestock. Slicing you through the marrow.

That's how I felt looking in the mirror that morning.

The guys in my head were in a frenzy. The strongest and most prominent leaders watched the big screen with stony faces, but the most passionate officials demanded a declaration of war. This was not uncommon. In the end, they'd always find a diplomatic solution that would get the greater Chance through the current crisis. All responses were well thought out, and the consequences were all projected. Future moves might be calculated. Due process reigned with more heft than any one of the guys, their passions or stoicism aside.

But something different happened that morning I awoke alone and naked in a veritable stranger's house to find my body defaced. It was almost as if those little guys convened in an emergency meeting and agreed that this body they occupied did indeed have value, regardless of how it was perceived externally. It was their temple. It was sacred. It was one of the only things on the planet that truly belonged to Chance Branch.

And it had been desecrated like the walls of an underpass.

After a unanimous vote, one of those little officials in my head—presumably the chairman, president, and commander-in-chief—pushed a red button that rendered an irreversible shift in policy. As result, the snapshot recollection of my mucus splattered on Trinity's face no longer mortified me. *Good*, I thought. *Maybe I'll do it again, but on purpose.* I was done living in fear of what others thought of me, or what they might do to me—after all, I was bigger than all of them. What did I have to fear? *Abuse?* What did I have to lose? My *pride?* But beyond that, this new doctrine decreed that I'd no longer source my pride from the meager offerings of the outside world. However humble this band of little dudes in my head might be, they'd circle the proverbial wagons and trust no one but each other with my self-worth.

I had no more fucks to give. The bold leader in my head enacted the Zero Fucks Doctrine, signified by a rousing speech that riled the masses.

I checked my front pocket and extracted my phone to discover an unprecedented and alarming number of notifications. Eight missed calls, a dozen text messages, three voicemails, and two failed inquiries from the family phone plan to pin my location. On any other day of my life, this would've filled me with exhilaration. To be the object of such concern to however many people would've inflated my flaccid ego to the point it might burst. But the lack of satisfaction it provided me further supported this new creed being ratified.

The calls were all from Mom and Dad, as were the voicemails and eleven of the twelve text messages. I chose to open the one text from someone else—Trinity.

> Hey lightweight! Looks like you couldn't hang, so we had a lil fun [punctuated by a laugh-cry emoji] Had to head off to work but will call u later [smooch emoji]

I scoffed. "*Lil fun*, huh?" I said out loud. If she tried to plant that smooch on me in person, I'd shove her face away hard enough to make a hole in the drywall with the back of her head. I went downstairs, leaving my shirt unbuttoned on the off chance Trinity's dad mustered the nerve to confront me about being there the morning after sleeping in his daughter's room. I rehearsed the snide reply I'd fire at him, putting a venomous twang in the way I said his name. Would I call him Roscoe in blatant insolence, or let my tone convey the ironic disrespect in the way I addressed him as *Mr. Smith?*

As I reached the landing and processed the words my mind uttered, a chilling thought forced me to freeze where I stood.

Smith?

Sure, it was the most common surname in America. But that alone wouldn't quash this nagging feeling. I scanned the vacant living room, resting my gaze on one of the picture frames lying on its face. With the same trepidation as though I were about to check the vital signs of a body I'd stumbled upon in the woods, I floated toward it with near certainty as to what I'd find. I picked it up, my jaw already clenched tight before my eyes confirmed my suspicions.

It was a posed, smiling family photo of Roscoe with Trinity hanging off of one shoulder, and Chip leaning on the other.

She's Chip's sister.

I'm not sure how long I leered at that photograph, but it was a while. I savored the hatred burgeoning inside me the way I might hold a shot of bad moonshine in my mouth before choking it down. I knew this was going to have a lasting effect on my sobriety, so I might as well bask in its nauseating effect. Masochistic, I know—but the response was autonomic.

In that state of mind, I was in no position to connect all the dots, but I didn't need to. Trinity's spell on me broke, and my awakening swept away the quixotic aura. What remained was a smoldering core of unadulterated wrath, distilled by decades of suffering and refined by the complex cocktail of hormones that had only recently been unearthed. The unstable combination unleashed a chain reaction to which I became but a witness.

I didn't make a conscious decision to slam the frame onto the floor with all my might, but I remember the shattering glass resonating with more gratifying richness than any music I'd ever heard. The cacophony rang like a war cry, as though one of those little guys in my head smeared markings on his face in his own blood and screamed it. The volatile crowd behind him roared in a cathartic fever pitch, and—in no uncertain terms—I completely lost my shit.

The lamp nearby became my first weapon of opportunity. I yanked it, and in one fluid motion pulled its cord from the wall socket and reached it behind my head in a backswing. Then I used it to swat the rest of the frames on the table with all the force in my big body. My rage fueled my rage, and before I could comprehend my actions—let alone their ramifications— half of the breakable objects in the room broke. I put five holes in the drywall before the lamp itself broke in half. I seethed, my shoulders heaving, in search of my next blunt object. Seeing nothing suitable, I lifted the fifty-five-inch LCD flat screen off the TV stand and hurled it through the picture window over the couch and into the bushes outside.

At that point, I can only characterize the rest of the episode as a blackout, because I remember nothing more of it. I do, however, know what the police report and ensuing civil suit would later disclose—over $8,000 in damages, including emotional duress and attorney's fees and court costs. However, the criminal charges of trespassing and disorderly conduct would be dropped as soon as the District Attorney became aware of my valid accusations that I'd been drugged and assaulted while in an unconscious state.

After my rampage, I sat in the middle of that destroyed room and called Dad to pick me up. As expected, he was displeased at being roused from his midday slumber, but that irritation somehow mutated into masculine pride by the time he pulled into the driveway. He wanted details as we pulled away, which I guarded for obvious reasons. But soon enough, in accordance with the Zero Fucks Doctrine, I misled him to think I'd lost my virginity to this nubile blonde, going so far as to show him the most provocative photos from Trinity's Instagram profile. In response to his palpably jealous probing, I decided to go all in with a lofty tale, fabricating salacious details I was fairly certain he'd retain for his own autoerotic purposes. The last two minutes of the drive home were silent, and I knew it was because this asshole—who may or may not be my biological father—was dying inside at hearing this. I held my hand over my mouth and kept my head turned to conceal the satisfied smile that wouldn't stay off of my face.

Of course, he'd later learn the truth. But by then, it wouldn't matter.

The panicked voicemails from him and Mom warmed my heart, even though their concern was shrouded in anger and threats of punishment. They were shit parents, but at least I knew they cared if I died.

My bar was low.

12

ONCE I CLEARED THE ONSLAUGHT OF NOTIFICATIONS IN MY phone that morning, I put my phone away in favor of a three-day bender playing World of Warcraft—maintaining my newfound maverick persona online, to fruitful outcomes. My fellow outsiders appreciated my rollicking leadership, and for the first time playing the game, that became my identity more than my lisp.

This retreat did, of course, get interrupted early on by a visit from the police, who informed my parents of the criminal allegations against me for the destruction of the Smiths' living room. I got a severe tongue-lashing, and endured an interrogation that caused my lies to multiply exponentially. By the end of the tale I wove, Todd had slapped Trinity, and I came to her rescue. Chip got mad that I put holes in their wall whilst pummeling Todd, so he and I came to blows as well. I fled through the front door, and the two of them heaved the giant TV through the front window, hoping to hit me with it (this part took a lot of explaining, and I don't think they bought it). It was actually somewhat liberating to spin a tale knowing that the truth would later surface. Lucky for me, the criminal charges were dropped, and we had nowhere near $8,000 to our name, so it was all moot.

But on the bright side, I didn't have to go to jail, and I could return to my fictional world of greatness. Those consecutive days and nights doing exactly what I wanted rejuvenated me just in time for the battle lurking over the horizon. My ignorance was indeed bliss—but more importantly, it provided me with the psychological and emotional rest I'd soon need.

The evening before the first day of senior year, I retreated to my room. *Warcraft* had pulled me away long enough, and it was time to prepare myself for reality. I got through this loathsome transition by reminding myself this would be the last year of school, and the end of my woes. All those detestable idiots would disappear from my life the moment I chucked my mortarboard into the sky. After this one last 180 days, I'd be able to play video games and waste away in fantasy for as long as I could retain my parents' support. Even if I had to take on a dead-end job to contribute financially until they croaked and endowed me with their meager inheritance, it would be a vast improvement over the arduous status quo I'd maintained for the last twelve years. However grueling this last mandatory academic push might be, my emancipation from it was nigh.

Mom got me a new shirt for the first day, upholding a rare tradition. Every year, regardless of whatever else was going on, she'd buy me a new shirt for the first day of school. I think it was her way of showing that she cared, but also her way of earning her right to wear the mother badge. She always took a picture of me wearing the new shirt and posted it to Facebook—like a critical assignment she dared not botch in light of her otherwise failing grade as a parent. This year's reveal of that teal Polo sobered me like a splash of cold water in the face.

Social media was never my thing, considering how centric it was around friendship, popularity, and vanity—none of which fit into my repertoire. But like so many of the things I hated, it was a requirement I endured. It'd become my own solitary custom the night before the first day to check the feed on Instagram and Snapchat, and even a Facebook scrub to see what everyone's parents were talking about. In conformity with social norms, I had a dormant profile on TikTok, so I checked that, too. Honestly, I found it all exhausting, despite the lack of effort I put into it. So that night, I checked Snapchat and Facebook first, then ended my obligatory research by checking Instagram.

I didn't know how algorithms worked (and I never will). Being the dork I am, you'd think I could speak geek and understand all that techy nonsense. But that would only illustrate your ignorance of the difference between a dork and a geek or nerd.

You see, geeks are the highest order of social rejects—quirky, endearing geniuses who have the potential to own the world, like icons such as Bill Gates or Mark Zuckerberg. They're what parents hope for upon realizing their kids will never be athletes or attract an adequate life partner via pure looks or charm. A step down from that were nerds, who would never quite reach *god* status, but still stood to make fortunes from their natural zeal for technological minutiae. Most parents accepted this bargain once coming to terms with their children's lack of global greatness.

However many levels down from that were people like me— dorks, chumps, and other phylum of socially inept losers with no intellectual advantage or marketable skills. This lowest caste of pariahs within which I fit—*the Untouchables,* so to speak— had about the same technical savvy as our parents, aside from our awareness of a few fleeting trends.

What I did know about social media logic was that these

applications had a robotic intelligence privy to the consuming public's tendencies. The bots know they have about fifteen seconds to grab our attention, and the analytics are written to capitalize within those parameters. Instagram employed such artificial minds, and thus, upon opening the app, immediately presented me with the most unsettling content at its disposal.

Trinity—who I'd forgotten I'd mutually followed—popped up first in the feed with a sepia-filtered picture of my naked body on her bed, marked up and slumped to one side. My pooch obscured my groin, allowing the days-old post to clear the platform's pornography scrub. Blackness closed in at the edges of my sight. Even as I lie on my side in bed, I worried I might faint seeing my own body on display, with 233 likes and eighty-nine comments, captioned only by the gutting hashtag, *#FatChance*.

Despite my lightheadedness, I sat up, my mouth agape. I clicked on Trinity's handle (which was *@trini_sweet_tea*—this bitch actually thought her sweet tea recipe set her apart from the masses). My attention first went to a video that was part of her "story."

I look back and laugh at how it's labeled that way. Her publication of my nude body is somehow *her* story, in social media vernacular. I suppose it's true, in that everything that happens affects everyone involved, but that content of my unconscious self wasn't hers. It was *mine*. It was *my* body, and a turning point in *my* life. That bitch was nothing but a pawn in *my* story.

But call it hers, Instagram. Whatever.

Against the advice of every little guy in my mind's operating committee, I found the video on her profile and checked the comments while Todd and Trinity giggled in the background in amusement at the markings they put on me. I'll spare what the comments said (for my own sake as much as anything else), but I will say they were all patently inhumane. Of all eighty-nine comments, only one user had the nerve to declare it wrong to humiliate another human being this way.

One.

Out of eighty-nine.

The top comment, which had twenty-one likes, was posted by none other than Chip Smith himself—I recognized his abhorrent likeness, even in the minuscule circle it occupied, before I noticed his Instagram handle, *@imchipsmithb1tch*. While they only confirmed what I'd already deduced, those eight words twisted the knife still firmly lodged in my back.

I owe you BIG for this one, sis ♥

The statement itself said quite enough in its simple brutality. But the heart emoji—ironically—expressed a whole other level of heartlessness. Brothers and sisters, especially those close in age and of the adolescent brand, are notoriously known to bicker. Yet this sadistic affront to my very humanity elicited a public display of their love and unity?

How could that make any sense to anyone?

But quite apparently, it did. The adrenaline buzz and tears inhibited my ability to read all five replies to his comment, but the gist translated to rampant applause for their coordinated efforts. As the tears rolled down my cheeks, the guys in my head marched with makeshift signs and yelled through bullhorns in cohesive support, shouting a message I'd never once considered throughout the torrent of cruelty that was my life.

There's nothing wrong with *me*.

They're the defective ones.

I tossed my phone and resolved to shake it off. I'd win by not letting them get to me, I told myself. As much as I meant that, I knew it was a pipe dream. They'd gotten to me. Big time. Perhaps to a necessary extent.

I didn't sleep a wink that night. How could I? While this may have been a contributing factor to my behavior that next day, I regret nothing. The sense of chaos made me feel like a roller coaster passenger—the only power I could wrest from the jaws of fate was the ability to foresee the next turn and plan for it. Powerless as this felt, I sensed an epiphany.

Just a few days before, the entirety of my mental energy had been devoted to the pursuit of a romance—even though I knew it to be unattainable in the wisest depths of my mind (one of those little guys undoubtedly walked around with a homemade T-shirt that said *I told ya so*). I'd never reach the cerebral tranquility necessary for sleep to reflect on that, knowing the whole thing was an elaborate ruse to disgrace me. The photo shoot, the uncle who scouts for Ole Miss, the goddamn papayas—*all* of it was a lie. *Of course it was.* Those intoxicating chemicals as I lay on the banks of the creek, staring at the trees with a new appreciation for the richness of their greens—all the product of a mirage. Would I ever feel that way again?

Did I even *want* to, after this?

This was all in addition to the routine anxiety associated with the night before the first day of school, so nothing was as delusional as my hope of falling asleep. Normally, I'd plan out how I'd find a way to lay low (at just under seven feet tall). I'd think about how I was going to get that goddamn P.E. credit, for real this time. It probably should've stayed top of mind, considering I wouldn't graduate without completing it this year. But all of these business as usual considerations fell to the bottom of the pile, given the current crisis at hand.

I did the math. There were about a hundred kids in my class, and Trinity's post had gotten more than double that in likes, probably ten times as many views. Chip would have made all of his own followers aware of this product of his devious machinations, but I hadn't checked his profile at all. It was safe to assume that many of his followers were classmates from whatever school he'd tormented obese kids at before coming to Chandler's Marsh, but I couldn't make a definitive guess. Nevertheless, despite so many unknown variables, I concluded that my whole class, the rising juniors, and some substantial portion of the underclassmen had seen Trinity's post, in addition to whatever other mortifying pictures or videos existed from that night. I considered scouring to see what other content existed, but the committee in my mind deemed it moot. Why do that to myself?

I devoted the rest of my sleepless energy to an action plan. Laying low was obviously more laughable than ever. The default option was to comply with the standing policy to suck it up and just get through the day, letting my psychological callouses absorb whatever mistreatment came my way. While this seemed an undesirable path, it had been the status quo for over a decade due to its achievable goal—just get through the day without letting them see me cry. There might be two or three kids remaining in town who'd been present the last time I cried at school. The back end of this plan promised the opportunity to cry it out once I got home, but I couldn't remember a time I ever did. By the time I made it to the last bell, my internal fortifications had always grown too impassable to access upon reaching emotional safety.

Over the many years of torment, I'd forgotten how to cry.

Regardless of history, this course of action wouldn't do. Even if it could enable me to survive the day, I didn't want it to. *Survival* dangled like a carrot in front of me, a reward I'd never truly redeem. What good would it be to continue living if this was all life had to offer? And if I made it through the day, I'd have to do it again. And again. And again.

No, thanks.

13

THE GUYS IN MY HEAD BREWED ANOTHER POT OF COFFEE and—with the leaders responsible for the failed *Shake It Off and Don't Cry* policy overthrown—wiped the whiteboards clean in favor of a novel scheme. The new steward sketched the brainstormed options, all of which called for stauncher defenses. I could prepare an arsenal of retorts for each taunt I anticipated. I could target my highest-profile tormenters with aggressive counterattacks, which would take the rest of the night to plot. I could swallow my pride and become a snitch, bringing every bully to justice before the principal until the rule of law restored order to my day—if such a thing ever existed.

As daylight tinted the blinds of my room, one of those guys who'd stayed quiet finally raised his hand and proposed something that made the whole room exchange pensive glances. Something that would change my life forever.

Of course.

It was exactly the hair-brained idea I (or was it *we?*) had been waiting for. The reenergized board room erupted in a flurry, shaking that guy by his shoulders, and I sat up in bed. I grabbed my phone and got started laying the groundwork. The dawn hours flew by as I worked with a dedication previously exclusive to video game obsession. When Mom poked her head in to wake me up, she found me already dressed and ready. She expressed concern that I'd been up all night gaming, and I promised her everything was fine. Just *fine.*

For once, that wasn't a total lie.

She walked away, and I held my phone up in selfie mode, tussling my sweaty, jacked-up hair. It didn't look right—and I mean that *beyond* the blind-monkey barbering with which my mother had bequeathed me. It just didn't fit with who I'd become, literally overnight. I went to the bathroom to take my morning dump, brush my teeth, and with that same rote confidence, shear the last of the bronze locks off of my scalp and into the bathtub. I toweled the clippings off of my bald head and ran my hand over it in the mirror, then did something I'm not sure I'd ever done before in earnest.

I stared back at my reflection and smiled.

I returned to my room, avoiding my mom—not out of shame, but urgency to execute my plan unabated. I closed the door, looked at my bald self on my phone's screen, and started recording.

"Welcome to the world according to the one and only Fat Chance," I said to my invisible audience.

And so began my catharsis. I turned the camera forward and walked through my house, calling out the nonfunctional air-conditioning unit in my parents' bedroom, then to my mom, who I said "loves me, but hates having to." Her protest could not have better illustrated what love looks like in the Branch household, so I captured it, untainted by further commentary. I did, however, respond when she asked about my shaved head by telling her I had to finish what she'd started.

In the midst of showing my following (which did not yet substantially exist) the trials of a giant living in a single-wide trailer, the man I referred to as "Mr. Branch" walked in the door after his overnight shift.

"The hell's all this about?" he chided, his face worn and twisted in a scowl. "Are you recording me? And since when do you call me *Mr. Branch?*"

"Since the other day, when you said you didn't believe I came out of your dick."

"Chance!"

"It's true, Ma. You should really hear Pops'—sorry, *Mr. Branch's*—theory. It's quite compelling. Look at him, and look at you. Now look at me. No DNA test necessary! The mill worker's research has already reached a conclusion. Ain't that right, *sir?*"

"Boy, turn that damn camera off," Mr. Branch commanded with a stern finger. He looked tired, as one would be at that stage of his waking day. I almost felt bad springing this on him, but that sympathy lasted only as long as it took to remember how much consideration he'd given me on the way to Trinity's house.

I stopped recording, and not only because my arm got tired—I'd gotten enough of this at-home content. Shorter videos were more likely to trend, anyway. Plus, my reckless word choice had left my screen covered in spittle spray, and I needed to wipe it clean. I bid both of my housemates a cheerful farewell, grabbed my backpack, and lumbered to the end of the gravel lot to await the bus. As the stubby orange vehicle rounded the bend, I resumed my video documentation, reminding my audience of the connotations associated with riding the short bus.

The doors clanked open, and I sidestepped up each of the stairs, then plopped my bag on the floor beneath the oversized seating compartment set aside just for me. I kept the video rolling and switched to selfie mode as I heard snickering near the back of the bus. One of them made a loud farting noise, and someone else said, "I heard he *ate* it."

"You see," I said in a hushed tone, like David Attenborough trying not to disturb the natural behavior of wild beasts. "When you look like me, even the *special* kids learn to make fun of you." I frowned at the camera. "Can you even imagine that?"

I went into passive mode, recording everything behind me and commenting only with facial expressions, most of which sought to convey *no big deal; this is typical.* My heart pounded as we neared the school, but not for the usual reasons. I couldn't wait to get there. This exposé already felt amazing, and I'd just gotten started.

Entering the school, I held the phone at eye level to ensure viewers could see how it all looked from that high up. Every face looked in my direction at once, like baby birds at the sight of their mother. Half of them turned away to feign disinterest and ridicule me on the sly instead. The rest kept staring, poorly hiding their laughs and smiles. I panned side to side with my phone, taking care to capture every single one of their ruthless asshole faces.

Activity hyped up, and the long hallway filled with hoots and shrieks. I kept my focus on the screen, viewing my world from a new lens—as someone else. One particularly large cluster of kids just a few paces ahead held the face I was looking for. I bumped my way through anyone between me and my target, stopping short, close enough to zoom in on Chip's face.

"This is Chip Smith, who'd be nothing without me to kick around. Ain't that right? Say hi to everyone, bitch—I mean, *Chip.*"

He flashed his eyebrows at my uncharacteristic and unimaginative jab, then fired his own. "*Everyone?* You mean all *two* of your followers?" He waited for his entourage's laughs to settle. "So, how was your summer, *Fat Chance?* Eat anything good?"

This time, I waited for the reaction to die down. "Oh, are you referring to the last day of school, when you shoved shit into my mouth? Or do you mean the other time, when you put a fucking gun in my mouth?" (This last one was an embellishment, but what was he gonna do—correct me?) I didn't filter my words to accommodate my lisp, as I'd become conditioned to do. If I happened to spray some spit in his face, all the better.

His smile faded, now resembling a grimace. "No idea what you're talking about, tubs."

Chip knew as well as anyone he'd be foolish to confess to criminal assault on the record, and my attempt to trick him into it served as a warning shot. His face reddened, except for one area on his left cheek—which remained his natural skin color. The first bell rang.

"Are you wearing makeup?" I said, pointing to the splotch. He walked away with his posse, and ignored me—which, to me, smelled of blood in the water. I kept pace behind him, until we all stopped at a snarl in the hallway traffic. Putting the camera in his face, I pointed at the spot again, which now looked even more pronounced. "What's this? Is that Maybelline? Or were you born with it?"

His face steeled, and before I could react, he slapped the phone out of my hand. The halls quieted quickly enough that I could hear my phone sliding down the hall.

Not my phone, I thought. *Not today, motherfucker.*

I may not have cared about anyone's perception of me anymore, but I wanted to document my experience, and my phone was the only tool at my disposal. Even in his ham-handed ignorance, he'd hit me where I was vulnerable.

For the last time.

Before I could plan my next move, I found both of my hands around Chip's neck, pushing him toward the lockers. His back slammed against them, loud as a gunshot, and I leaned into my grip. I could feel the brittleness of his windpipe, so I let up just enough not to crush it. I bent down, speaking so only he could hear me.

"I'm bigger than you," I whispered. "I can *end you.*"

Chip sneered, doing his best to appear calm while every blood vessel in his face bulged. I savored the sensation and tried to record the moment in my mind, for my own viewing pleasure. His feigned calm broke as his eyes protruded, starting to glaze over. He dropped his books to slap my arms—not as a defensive fighting technique, but in a show of submission. He was tapping out.

"Oh, you want mercy?" I said, my tone making it clear clemency wasn't coming. A few girls around me pleaded to release him. While I had no interest in appeasing them, I knew their panic would draw the attention of a teacher or other authority figure, most of whom were in their classrooms. I released him just as the second bell rang.

He looked at me from under his brow without tilting his head up. I couldn't tell whether he was trying to shoot me a crazy, serial-killer glare, or if his neck just wasn't working properly. Either way, I answered with a tight smile. Then, as he squatted down to pick up his books, he keeled over like a toppling statue, again banging into the lockers. He lay unconscious, his arms still sticking out like a zombie's, twitching every few seconds.

I looked around, at last concerned I'd gone too far. To my left, I saw an empty hallway, except for one faceless student behind a locker, holding up her phone to record the ordeal. I couldn't identify her in the chaos, but I knew it was a girl wearing some kind of weird poof ball on top of her head. To the right, Ms. Loganberry tapped toward us on her high heels, rushing to Chip's aid. She checked his pulse, then glanced back at me and asked what happened. I shook my head and shrugged hard, saying that we'd been talking, and Chip went to pick his books up and just passed out. I looked left again—no one there.

Feeling the clock ticking, I said I was late and excused myself. I backtracked to my homeroom, squatting to pick up my phone on the way. When I checked behind me, Chip was propped up against the lockers, relaying his version of the incident— whatever that might be—while Ms. Loganberry fanned his face with a planner. I ducked into homeroom without confrontation, and sat in my seat.

Sweaty and panting, I tried to wrap my head around what had just happened. Homeroom buzzed with chatter about me, but I could sense a different tone than usual. They weren't whispering insults about my physique or otherwise shaming me. They were gossiping about what I'd done.

I started to wonder how much trouble I was in—with Chip, the administration, or anyone else. I'd already been named in a police report, and crossed a kid who'd once threatened me with a large gun. Even if he refused to snitch, *someone* in that hallway would turn against me and reveal that I was the cause of Chip's collapse. What if I'd seriously hurt him? There was no chance I'd get away with it. Would I do time? Someone had gotten me on video—that girl in the hall. Panic began to set in before one of the guys in my head pounded the gavel and returned my thinking to order.

What can I do about it now? I thought, taking a deep breath.

Nothing.

Across the room, I caught Seth Charles leering at me as though he'd been waiting for me to notice him. I shot him a casual *what's-up* nod (nodding up once—not to be confused with the more cordial *how's-it-going* nod, which is one downward nod). Once the teacher noted his presence, he crouch-walked toward my seat and squatted next to me, begging for details of the confrontation. After I answered several questions about what exactly had transpired, he hit me with a more open-ended inquiry.

"The hell's gotten into you, bro?"

I shrugged. "Sick of his shit, man. Guess I just decided to remind him that I can break him."

He wheezed a laugh and slapped me hard on the shoulder, and scurried back to his assigned seat. This may not seem like much, but knowing Seth the way I did, that was a monumental show of admiration. Any regrets brewing about my actions dissipated, and I returned my mind to the primary task.

Momentum was on my side. As a heavy person, I knew how valuable that could be.

14

I ENSURED MY PHONE WAS INTACT, AND PREPARED TO RECORD again when I reached my first class, which was math with Mr. Dorchester. His classroom had my special desk at the front and off to the side—among my least favorite orientations. Kids are extra brutal when their target is sitting right in front of them. The fact that my side profile reveals some of my most unflattering attributes only exacerbated their temptation. Taking that seat would typically fill me with dread, but today it was perfect. I wanted to capture my experience in its rawest forms, down to the finest idiosyncrasies, and this would illustrate several of them. I couldn't wait.

The bell rang, and I reentered the anarchy of the Chandler's Marsh High School hallway, phone up and recording. Where I would normally keep my head down and apologize for bumping into people who knew they were in my way, I altered my path for no one. I dwarfed them all. They'd mocked me for my size, so it was only fair that they get the hell out of my way because of it. I met everyone's eyes like the Terminator, assessing whether it was worth my time to confront them or let them pass without incident.

My vision locked in—still much like the Terminator—on a peculiar image. I could almost see the superimposed outline form around Ray Mack and Candace Klauss as they huddled near a locker, both engrossed in their phones.

I had a lot going on and couldn't get distracted, but this jarred me. Why would one of my two friends be in such close conversation with the one and only girl I'd ever viewed as a potential object of affection? Was he into her? Or she him? Was this some sort of instant karma for growing a backbone and displaying a shred of aggression?

I decided I'd go crazy trying to figure it out with the little information at my disposal, so I repelled the image from my mind. I walked into math class and took my seat, keeping my phone covertly pointed at the rest of the class under the tabletop. Math began—and on day one of classes, I knew instruction to be lightweight, so I kept my focus on recording. Perhaps it was Murphy's Law in effect, or perhaps my singular show of fortitude had shifted the paradigm, but I captured nothing noteworthy all period long. None of them pointed, mocked, giggled, or whispered. Many waited for the opportunity to text, and did so in a rush. They weren't hiding anything from me—just from Mr. Dorchester. They were most likely tapping their keyboards about what I'd done to Chip, and I knew it. That wasn't the content I was after, so I stopped trying to capture it.

Western Civilization with Mr. Foley was next. I made it to class without further incident, and I didn't even see Chip in the hallway for the second consecutive transition. Did he go home? To the hospital? Was he *dead?* The possibilities excited and terrified me all at once.

My special seat at a card table sat at the back of the room for Mr. Foley's class. I took my place and recorded everything, but the camera drifted off to the side as I noticed Candace come in. But not only did she have the same class for the same period, she met my gaze for an extended duration before taking a seat close enough that I could smell her. (You know—if I was creepy like that . . . which I'm not.)

Just as a reminder, my direct interactions with Candace were less common than solar eclipses. Those three seconds of eye contact probably matched the elapsed time we'd looked into each other's eyes over the course of a decade. My heart doubled pace for a stint for that reason, in addition to the fact that she looked especially pretty today. She wore mascara and had her hair tied up in some intricate, messy knot on the top of her head. Her flowy dress caught my interest, despite its modesty. To top this fashionable entrance off, she took her seat and pulled the tie from her tightly bound hair, allowing it to burst like a grenade and cascade down her back.

Mr. Foley started rambling, which, as per usual, had nothing to do with world history. On par with years prior, he opened class by talking about his daughter, who played volleyball at Mizzou, and that led to more of his tangential soliloquy about the intricacies of collegiate volleyball. Like my classmates, my eyelids grew heavy. Just before I prepared to stop recording and stow my phone, I got a notification that someone wanted to airdrop a large file to me.

Airdrop—a feature exclusive to iPhone users—allowed files to be transferred from one Apple device to another, based on physical proximity. In order to receive a file, I needn't be in the sender's contact list. The only requirement on my end was for my phone to be set to receive files from anyone, which it was. (I should mention, this wasn't the default setting. When I'd gotten my phone, I set it this way to introduce the infinitesimal possibility of errantly receiving a file meant for someone else. Because why wouldn't I?)

This feature required me to accept or decline the request, and I chose the obvious. The twenty or so seconds of this transfer tortured me, because I couldn't imagine what was being sent to me, or who'd sent it. And of course, twenty seconds is plenty of time for a feral imagination. I looked around the class. The questions ricocheted like high-powered bullets in a steel room.

Was this another taunt? If so, how would I capture it for my story? If not, what could it be? What could the file possibly be, if it wasn't among the dirt already publicly aired? Why would this happen now, of all times? How could anyone in this class know which mobile number was mine? Neither Seth nor Ray were in this class, and I couldn't imagine who else would know my number.

At the end of those twenty seconds, I hid my phone screen with the adeptness only my generation can, and pressed play to see a different version of me. The viewpoint was that of whoever had been off to my left, recording me slamming Chip against the locker.

I still cringed at the sight of my enormous form, even though I'd seen myself in much more unflattering conditions—as had at least half the student body. I think most people are put off by how they look from any perspective other than head-on in the mirror, but it's worse for people like me, who hate even that reflection. Every pudgy roll, every badly fitting section of clothing, and every frame of reference only amplifies the self-loathing for big people. But once the shallow shame passed, I saw another glaring difference from this rare viewpoint.

I looked fucking *fearsome.*

Not to be vain, but ferocity looked damn good on me. And not to denigrate myself, but seeing myself in such a raw state reminded me of a circus elephant. Put a headdress on it, drape it in gaudy attire, have some puny handler lead it around for the amusement of others, and it seems but a harmless object present solely for everyone's amusement. But watch what happens when a circus elephant snaps. It looked just like that. Watching the replay, I saw the way Chip flinched as I lunged at him. How quickly the halls cleared—some kids dropped papers and never looked back. I rewound the footage before it even reached the end, savoring the scattering crowd a couple more times. I wished I could turn the sound up to hear the hush following the clash of Chip's spine against the metal lockers. I let it play through, and watched his comical collapse.

After a few more replays, something else stood out. Whoever recorded this hadn't budged the entire time. When that swarm of kids scurried off like cockroaches after the lights come on, the video frame didn't flinch. It didn't shake, twitch, balk, or otherwise betray any sign of unease. The person recording was still and unafraid. This perspective came from someone who had the mettle to stick around for my little moment of redemption, when no one else did. Someone either brave, or at the very least, undaunted by me—even after this violent display.

An admirer, even?

I closed the file and looked up, mostly to avoid being called out by Mr. Foley (despite his wandering monologues, he had a knack for spotting a distracted pupil). Just as my eyes locked onto a blank spot on the whiteboard, my peripheral vision caught sight of Candace Klauss turning her head and tossing her hair around. Just as I turned my focus onto her, she glanced back and met my eyes. I let my jaw fall and leaned back, smiling.

As though she'd been busted committing some sort of crime, she whipped her head forward, and hunched. I stared at the backs of her arms, watching them turn a splotchy pink.

It was her. It *had* to be her.

I knew there was a reason I'd always liked her. Okay . . . numerous reasons.

Class crawled by, slowed by my eagerness to follow Candace out and talk to her. But when the bell finally rang, she booked it without looking back. I thought about shouting her name, but bit my tongue upon remembering the unseen spotlight trained on me at all times. I could contact her discreetly now that I had her number—there was no need to rope her into my shit show.

I went to my next classes, recording as much as I could without having my phone confiscated. I pondered sending Candace a text, maybe just saying thank you, but decided against it. Now would be the worst time to get sidetracked from my principal objective. After powering through art and English classes, the next promising opportunity for viable content arrived: lunchtime.

15

AS ONE MIGHT IMAGINE—BUT NEVER REALLY THINK ABOUT— lunch period is unbearable for an overweight kid. On one hand, everyone assumes you're a fat pig who's eager to overeat, and they'll watch your every move, waiting for the prime snapshots of ridicule. On the other hand, you are hungry, and your normal food intake is greater than the skinny kids. Worst of all, lunch is the only period promising anything resembling pleasure, but you're tasked with eating daintily, like it isn't the highlight of your day. Lunch period is by far the best, but also a close second for worst, next to P.E.

But for my purposes that day, lunch was a golden opportunity to capture the essence of being Fat Chance for whatever following I might dredge up. As expected, I could feel the typical pointing and smack talk all around me. My problem was one that Erwin Schrödinger articulated in 1935—that the phenomenon I aimed to prove the existence of would disappear the instant I tried to record it (Ray Mack explained this to me five times before I understood—you're better off hitting up Wikipedia). I panned my phone around the cafeteria while in the lunch line and from my seat, but the assholes would all break into feigned casual conversation with the lens upon them. The operation was a complete bust. I ceased recording and turned my full attention to my food.

Halfway through my first order of fries, another precedent shattered as Seth Charles slid his tray down and slapped my back entirely too hard, plopping down beside me. I always sat alone. It was a universal constant. Upheaval of this norm set the cosmos into disorder, and I felt like the lunchroom glitched upon observing this.

"I know this seat ain't taken!" he said, followed by a snort. He settled in and stuffed his mouth full of tater tots without shame. "You heard Chip went home, right?" he said through a stuffed mouth.

I stopped chewing. "Say what, now?"

"Yeah," he said, nudging my elbow with his. "His *daddy* had to come get him. I hear he was feeling woozy when they took him to the nurse. They was gonna call the ambulance, but Chip begged 'em not to. Sandy Freeman was in the office, and said he was 'bout crying, begging them to just let him go home. Then his daddy showed up, piss drunk. Sandy said he could barely walk, reeking of booze. Boy, I'll tell ya. That whole family's a hot mess."

I stared off into space. "No shit?"

"Just telling ya what I heard."

With that, I had a companion at lunch—a first after three years of high school. Seth probed for particulars about my attack on Chip, and I answered as honestly as I could. Passersby slowed more than once, indiscreetly lingering to soak up what they could of the details. I was front-page material for the first day of my senior year. It felt like a fantasy.

The thought of Chip falling from grace so swiftly shook me, vindicating as it was. It amounted to more than I could absorb in the moment, so I tabled it to relish later. And I would most certainly relish it. I'd watch that video for hours, as soon as I had the chance.

Other than that, lunch passed without incident. And unfortunately for my mission, so did the rest of the school day. Even P.E. was relatively eventless, with most of the time dedicated to covering the new protections in each of the sports we'd play throughout the semester. Apparently, an overzealous dodgeball incident from last year led to a parental complaint, which in turn mandated Mr. Nagy to introduce some semblance of order to his class. Which meant no more dodgeball.

There was one point in P.E. when I managed to record a snippet I knew I'd make use of. Todd—the supposed photographer Trinity had commissioned—shared this class with me. He refused to look my way at any point, but I made sure to zero in on him and narrate his part in my coordinated humiliation. I didn't know or care how much notoriety my eventual social media propagation would gain. This documentary was nothing more than a testimony of the truth. And this punk ass wanted to act like I wasn't in the room? I thought not. So I made sure to zoom in on his face and state his name for posterity.

If you're gonna be an asshole, at least be an asshole with a spine.

Dismissal was also disappointingly smooth, devoid of the routine mockery I had every right and reason to expect. It occurred to me that this new tactic of recording everyone might only make their derision more surreptitious. While this would lighten my day-to-day psychological load at school, it wouldn't serve my broader agenda of shining a light on my struggle as a human being in a cruel society. But all things considered, I guessed I'd take the wins where I could find them. And there was always tomorrow.

At home, after telling Mom that my first day was—of course—*fine*, I retired to my room to compile the footage I'd gathered in my day as a documentarian. I tried my hand at video editing, splicing, and effects, then staged my arsenal of truth to be launched. I wondered if I should wait until midnight for dramatic effect, or just go ahead and hit the check mark.

Opting for the latter, I posted five separate videos to Instagram. I made sure to tag Chip, Todd, and Trinity in each of them, and of course, capped them all with the hashtag *#FatChance*. Then I moved on to TikTok, where I knew I stood a much better chance of gaining traction with strangers in the digital abyss. But less than an hour into trying to figure that out, I got a notification that I'd gained a new follower on Instagram.

@candacecommandus started following you, it said.

I knew it was Candace Krauss, and I knew I should wait before following back. It's protocol. Even if my eagerness weren't secret, I'd never want anyone to know I'm engrossed in my phone 89 percent of my waking life, even though that's what we all see each other doing 100 percent of the time. I bucked that custom, and immediately requited her follow.

The next alert came only moments later, also from Instagram, notifying me that I'd been tagged in the comments of a video posted by Candace. I clicked on it, and up popped her video of me manhandling Chip Smith. The brief caption only read, "knight smites knave. gramercy!" I scrolled down to find that it had 377 likes.

It'd been posted less than an hour ago.

MY HEARTBEAT SLOWED, BUT WHOOSHED THROUGH MY ears. I tried to do the mental math to figure out the rate at which the like count on Candace's post was growing, but couldn't. My adrenaline rush and mathematical ineptitude wouldn't allow it.

I checked my posts, which had a cumulative three likes, then went back to Candace's. Then, perplexed by this disparity, I went to her profile. It took only a few seconds to deduce that she had an immense following, all because she was some kind of cosplay enthusiast. The number was expressed as a decimal in the thousands—*10.9K followers*. Her profile was littered with images of her in a shiny bustier, purple velvet capes, and crowns (or tiaras—as if I know the difference), surrounded by nerdy dudes wearing chainmail, plate armor, feathered helmets, and quite often, an excessive amount of body fat.

Without hesitation, I clicked the button to send Candace a direct message. Formalities be damned—I needed to capitalize on this hidden power of hers. My message rambled, and I probably should've proofread it, but I worried I'd chicken out if I did. As it went, this is the message I sent:

> Hey Candace. Pretty sure your the one that airdropped me the video of me choking Chip out

> lol… if so thx for that! I just wanna ask, would you mind adding the hashtag #fatchance to your post? I'm trying to trend a story about being overweight at this shit school. I can tell you about it later but I was hoping you could add the hastag now lol

I rubbed my forehead as some infighting broke out among the guys in headquarters about the quality of this communique to Candace. But it didn't matter—messages could be unsent, but she'd be able to see I deleted it, which opens a whole new host of faux pas to deal with. Nothing to do now but wait. If she added the hashtag, it might trend. And if it did, my posts—both present and future—could reach an unknown population of non-followers. That was the first step to gaining traction online, and Candace held the key. Maybe she'd ask me to solve a riddle or slay a mythical dragon to gain passage to this next level. I wasn't too proud to play along. Whatever happened next, I was all about it. I zoned out, fantasizing about how I'd look in chainmail and a tin helmet.

Nothing happened within my predetermined span of attention (about fifty-five seconds), so I returned to Candace's video. In the time it took to send that message, pine over it, regret it, and return to the feed, her post had grown to 987 likes.

Almost thrice what it'd been only *seconds* ago. Okay, minutes. But, like, *two* minutes.

With nothing else to do while I awaited her reply—which I had no choice but to hope was on its way—I went to the comment section to see what everyone was saying. Everything was phrased in medieval, chivalrous diction, so it took forever for me to translate each one. I'd never liked Shakespeare, whoever wrote King Arthur, or any of that middle-ages monarchy crap. The idea that a whole segment of the human population fixated on this perplexed and frustrated me throughout my desperate attempt to gather intelligence from the comment section.

What the hell is a knave, anyway? Is gramercy a good thing? Smite means to kill, right? After osmosing what I could via context, I gathered that Candace's *fair affinity*—or following— had some prior knowledge of Chip's misdeeds, and they were happy to see him thwarted. I also learned many of them thought I'd make a fine bailiff for any of the lords or ladies at the next festival, which would be a jousting tournament up in Kingdom City. One of them referred to me as an enraged ogre, which drew a backlash from several other users. I nearly crushed my phone's screen giving every one of those comments a like.

I went back to see if maybe I'd missed her reply to my message, but still nothing. She hadn't even read it. I did, however, see a slew of new notifications. I checked to find I had thirteen new followers. I perused the list and recognized a couple of them as users whose comments I'd liked.

Was that all it took?

To test this hypothesis, I went back to the comments section and looked for one to reply to. It seemed a crap shoot, so I decided to reply to Candace's comment where she'd just tagged me. My medieval phrasing was rough, but I figured I should speak in the parlance of the masses rather than come off like an out-of-place oaf. It took a few googles, but I thought it rang authentic enough to hit the send button.

> @candacecommandus thank you for scribing my duel, m'lady!

I immediately regretted my word choice, but let it stand anyway. Sure, it sounded cheesy and contrived, but that's how I perceived their whole silly dialect. Within seconds, likes and replies rolled in. Most of them were words and emojis of praise, but a couple felt the need to correct my broken attempt at the dialect. I wanted to clap back, but I chose to chalk it up to learning that a duel is something else entirely, and that the right way to address Candace was *her grace, her greatness,* or *her highness*—not *m'lady*. For reasons.

All this excitement had distracted me from the fact that I was starving, thirsty, and had to pee. My phone was also dying, so I put it on the charger and made my rounds in the bathroom and kitchen. By the time I got situated back on the bed with my snacks, drink, and phone, I discovered I'd gained over a hundred new followers. One hundred forty-four, actually—not that I was counting.

I stopped chewing and stared at my screen. I might've stopped breathing, too, which would explain the lightheadedness while sitting.

Opening up TikTok, I searched for Candace, to see if I could ride her coattails on an even hotter platform. There were no obvious hits when I looked her up by name or her Instagram handle, so I just started following any Candace I found at random, intending to weed out the impostors later.

Mom interrupted my research for supper, which I tore through like a ravenous dog. Dad—I mean, *Mr. Branch*—reprimanded me for it, but there was nothing in our unspoken tenancy agreement requiring me to eat slowly, so I ignored him. Mom went on about how badly I wore a shaved head, then probed for details about the first day of school. I stonewalled her with responses of *fine* and *alright* through loaded mouthfuls until my plate was clean, then hustled back to my room. She popped in a few minutes later— suddenly, like she'd hoped to catch me in whatever act—only to find me engrossed in my phone, not startled in the least.

I have a life now, Ma. *Gah.*

After uploading a couple of snippets to TikTok, the rest of

the evening was spent watching my online persona grow. My Instagram following rose to quintuple what it'd been for years, and each of my videos accumulated double-digit likes. But aside from that, only a few people bothered to comment, and my TikTok posts remained dormant. Worst of all, Candace still hadn't messaged me back, and I felt a black hole forming in my gut. It wouldn't be long before I imploded.

Had the *#FatChance* trend fizzled out before it'd even started?

I thought about sending Candace a text message since I now had her number. The debate in my headquarters was fierce—surely, the guys in my head had resorted to physical attacks, and some had to be escorted out by security. Those in favor of texting Candace rested their case on the limited time I had left to continue trending online. They felt it overshadowed the relatively insignificant risk of appearing desperate in her eyes. But the other camp argued clingy behavior risked scaring her off entirely—and permanently, while also jeopardizing her turning her royal subjects away from me.

Sometime after midnight, I turned off the lights and went through the motions of going to bed, knowing full well I'd never achieve sleep with my mind churning at full throttle. I turned off my phone's push notifications—except for Instagram direct messages—and closed my eyes. My fantasies wandered back and forth from reality, sometimes getting stuck in the real world. This was new for me. Reality had always sucked, and naturally repelled my subconscious. Fantasizing about the plausible just wasn't in my skill set. Just as I resigned to another sleepless night, my phone whistled. *Yoo-hoo!*

An Instagram message.

I tweaked a back muscle in my haste to retrieve my phone,

causing me to wince and pause. As soon as I powered through the pain, I snatched my phone and confirmed it was Candace's reply, then opened the message. I stared at her words for ten seconds.

Lol ok

That's it? I thought. *Didn't I give her a bunch of stuff to address?*

I reread my own message and realized that nothing explicitly demanded a response except my request for the hashtag. While this was fair, I thought broaching the topic of her airdrop and the video she'd posted was a reasonable expectation. Regardless, I went back to her post to find that she had indeed added the *#FatChance* hashtag to her caption. Not much else had changed since I last checked, so I chucked my phone to the floor and rolled over, groaning through the newborn pain in my back.

Only then did exhaustion catch up with me. The moment I closed my eyes, the sun came up, and my alarm sounded. I hit snooze a few too many times, apparently, because the next thing I knew, Mom was yelling at me to get up. There was barely time to bolt a couple of waffles down my gullet and get dressed, let alone fit in my morning dump, when I'd normally check my phone.

At the bus stop, I found a moment to check it, and my home screen was flooded with notifications. I had two text messages from unknown numbers, three Instagram messages, and too many Snapchat alerts to count—the number rose before my eyes. Most peculiarly, I also had Twitter notifications, which never happened—Twitter was like Facebook for people with way more time to waste on the opinions of strangers. Not really my thing.

I opened Instagram first and checked the messages. Of the

three, only Candace's mattered.

Looks like u got what you wanted lol

I did, did I?

It took just a few seconds of sifting through the notifications to realize there were too many to keep up with. I opened Twitter to find my video—complete with the *#FatChance* hashtag—had been shared by a user I'd never heard of, and retweeted by their followers en masse. Only then did I notice the Facebook notifications, oblivious to the bus idling right in front of me until the air brakes hissed and the doors opened.

The ride to school was more like a teleport. The preoccupation with my burgeoning fame ran deeper than vain obsession. I needed to sort out as much as possible to determine just how big this was. Would I be the main topic of conversation at school? How would I be received? What were those assholes all saying online about this? After everything they'd said and done to me over the years, how would they respond to this candid take of my life? For some frame of reference, I checked my Instagram videos. They each had over five hundred likes, and a mind-blowing fifteen thousand views. The one Candace recorded now had nearly *thirty thousand likes*.

My mouth hung open so long I drooled on my phone's screen.

The guys in my head gawked at their screens as well, trying to make sense of these numbers with such intensity that they had no record of the commute to school at all. I gazed out the window, watching the school draw nearer, while the guys failed to comprehend two words blaring like an alarm throughout every office in the headquarters.

I'm viral.

17

THE UNLOADING AREA OF THE SCHOOL WAS PACKED, WHEREAS on any other day, it'd only be occupied by however many kids stepped off a bus or two. Carpool kids and earlier bus kids must've all loitered in the unloading area, presumably waiting for my bus to arrive. The kids on the short bus with me seemed oblivious to my viral fame, and thus made uneducated assumptions confirming my suspicions.

"Is there a fight?"

"Are the news people here?"

"Maybe there's a celebrity at school today."

Oh, there's a celebrity at school alright, Earl. And he's sitting right in front of you.

I sat in stage fright while the other kids got off. It was all I could do. I froze. The guys in my headquarters second-guessed the scheme that'd come to fruition, denouncing it as one that would only have been successful if it had failed. Because then I could've said I tried. I'd have bared my soul and become a martyr for it. But now, as I ogled at that mob of meerkats with their eyes fixed on my bus like a predator on the horizon, I prepared to face the consequences of my unlikely success.

This is what I wanted, right? But what the hell was I supposed to do *now?*

It didn't matter. At that point, I had as much choice as a man in shackles on death row. I'd premeditated this act, and now I'd face justice—be it good or bad for me. Somehow, I'd thought things weren't hard enough before, being unavoidably noticeable in this obscure town. Now I held the same status in any place occupied by people born after the internet. I did it to myself; so I stood up, grabbed my bag, and descended the steps—my own little Green Mile. (Funnily enough, the bus's aisle actually was a shade of green.)

I don't know what I'd expected, but I know what I *didn't* expect: exactly what happened. The crowd erupted in feverish cheering and hollering, as though I'd just returned from a mission to Mars.

Many of my classmates recorded me during this moment, which would later reveal to me how dumb my face looks when I'm trying to make sense of something. I'm always cognizant of my lisp, but I sometimes forget it's a mere symptom of my oversized tongue, which protrudes in moments like this. I honestly don't think I could've looked dumber if I'd tried. (There was a point in watching these lesser-known clips that I considered claiming to have made that face on purpose. I opted instead to will them into obscurity by saying nothing. Probably wise.)

Starting that morning, I always joked that a funny thing happened to time as I fell asleep the night before. Perhaps my great mass, plugged into Einstein's theory of general relativity, could explain it in some scientific way. Still, I believed I did something to the space-time continuum that night. Mass times exhaustion, divided by the square root of my frustration, all squared by the number of followers I'd gained, rendered time as I knew it infinitesimal. If time flies when you're having fun, then it exceeds the speed of light when you have no idea what the fuck is going on.

The whole day elapsed in a blur. Not garbled like a drunken stupor, but strobed, like childhood. It was filled with significant events, but far too many to recall in retrospect. The remainder is an album of flashbulb moments. Candace giving me a high-five in passing, as though we'd been lifelong friends. Seth and Ray trailing me like shadows, sitting with me at lunch like it were some time-honored custom. Pats on the back from underclassmen and perfect strangers as I strode the halls, wielding the new bravado I'd found like a gun discovered in my dad's underwear drawer. A surreal heart-to-heart with Mr. Ogle, my English teacher, who revealed to me that he'd struggled with obesity before joining the army, and had experienced my plight firsthand. I also recall biting my tongue during this exchange. There's a world of difference between getting picked last in gym and being seen as a different species. His sentiment wasn't lost on me, though, so I nodded and flashed my eyebrows like a good active listener. Perhaps someday hypnosis will help me pluck more specifics from those eight hours.

The hard days in the dungeon were long and dark, but the hard-earned day in the limelight was as quick and blinding as a bolt of lightning.

One other detail from that day did stick out to me, but only after I made it back home and had a solid hour on the john to reminisce.

All day, I hadn't seen Chip Smith. Not even once. I hadn't even seen any of his cronies huddled together like they so often were. As if the forces of evil had been expelled from my domain.

Granted, Chip certainly wasn't the type to strive for perfect attendance. But I couldn't recall a single reprieve from his presence in the building all of junior year. I hadn't seen him in two full school days now, and none of the explanations for his uncharacteristic absence put my mind at ease.

Had I injured him more severely than intended? Was he hospitalized? Was he plotting some horrific revenge? Any and all of these could very well be, and would be disastrous. The pieces were all there. I began to unpack the Dateline episode of my own impending murder, reverse engineering the trace evidence homicide detectives would follow to solve the mystery, soon enough.

After enjoying a full year as the apex predator in a podunk Missouri community, Chip had become the object of the internet's disdain as a result of my deliberate action. Based on his past behavior, he clearly had no moral boundaries or reverence for the rules of engagement. I'd originally become his nemesis for doing nothing to him besides being obese and occupying his field of view. Now I'd usurped his power, and become the aggressor.

Motive.

On one occasion, he'd threatened me with a huge handgun. He also had a sister devious and heartless enough to collude with him, exhibiting proud disregard for human decorum, along with at least one friend—Todd—obviously cut from the same cloth. Three henchmen accompanied him when he fed me my own excrement. He had known weapons and accomplices at his disposal.

Means.

Chip could find me anytime he wanted, just like anyone else with functional vision in Chandler's Marsh. Established co-conspirators could easily supply him a false alibi, or create a diversion to catch me alone. His threat of retribution loomed constantly.

Opportunity.

The possibility of my own homicide swelled in my mind as entirely plausible, frustrating my ongoing effort not to panic.

AFTER TWO FULL DAYS OF FAR TOO LITTLE SLEEP, DREAMLIKE levels of fame, and an unaddressed detachment from my very origins, the prospect of foreseeing my own murder began to have severe physiological effects. At one point, I had a mini-breakdown on the john. Sweating profusely, my ass slid on the seat like it was a frozen pond. I ran my hands over my stubbly scalp, wondering how long this cranium would remain intact and devoid of a gaping gunshot wound. There was always the option of calling the cops preemptively. But I stared at the non-emergency number I'd looked up, never daring to thumb the send button.

My will to live amazed me at times. So many people struggle with depression, but among those people, none of them looks like me. None of them lived where I lived, or experienced a life quite like mine. None of them hated every moment of life more than I had, unless we all reached the maximum limit. If anyone had a damn good reason to consider suicide, it was teenage Chance Branch. Yet I never did.

Depression and circumstance do not go hand in hand. If they did, you wouldn't be reading this.

There's a fine but distinct line between depression and despair. One is clinical, and one is situational. While mine always felt clinical, it's also true I've always been a six-foot-ten ginger. So how could I know? All I know is that living in despair is depressing, and I've felt that way all my life.

When you hate who you are at the core, that's depression. I'd always assumed I hated myself. But until I became the darling of the anonymous internet, I didn't understand that in reality, I really just hated the five senses of everyone who perceived me.

My despair, while temporary, was legitimate. I was desired on this earth by no one—before today, anyway (unless my disillusioned football admirers count, which they shouldn't). Even my parents resented my existence, as evidenced by their proclivity to put literally any other priority over showing me a morsel of appreciation, validation, or—God forbid—affection. The denial of a definitive father was but the icing on this cake of sadness. With so many reasons to fall into hopelessness, I'd never once struggled to find cause to live. (Blizzard Entertainment may have something to do with this, since *World of Warcraft* often supplied those reasons, and they should be commended for preserving my life.)

Some of us get our asses kicked by the chemicals inside us. The rest get reduced to our lowest selves by the external chemicals available to us. For me, it was a healthily unhealthy mixture.

I gladly took in copious portions of salt, sugar, and fat, knowing full well the damage they'd all do to my long-term and short-term health. Dopamine is a hell of a drug. But don't mistake self-destructive behavior for a death wish. I ate all that stuff on a consistent basis because it's delicious, and everyone knows it—it's not even up for debate. Ask any chef. The secret to amazing food is always fat, sugar, and salt.

My world was shit. I needed some regular supply of happy endorphins and neurotransmitters, like any other member of the human race. Just because the source of my short-term happiness happens to perpetuate my long-term physical decline says nothing about my willingness to exist. Like all living things, I yearn to be fat and happy. I will not be judged harshly for getting a slim majority of that job done.

I never wanted to die, despite hearing so loudly that I should. Bitch that life might be, I treasured it. I'd never been able to list the reasons why, but I shouldn't have to. I'm here because, at some point in the process of natural selection, I earned the right to live. I had no desire to forfeit my reward for that achievement, nor relinquish it to another—in my humble opinion—lesser being.

Chip likely wanted me dead, and I couldn't be convinced otherwise before I departed from my bathroom that afternoon. I paced my room, unconcerned with my internet stardom, sweating from the stifling heat and the catastrophic demise awaiting me around any corner, at any time now. My life had grown bigger than itself, and gained steam like an oversized ship hurtling full speed ahead through a blinding fog. Every instinct told me to throttle back before I ran aground.

Should I apologize to him?

This question sickened me, in that any answer felt like a heavyweight punch to the gut. If I told Chip I was sorry, my own misdeeds would supersede his, which would be unequivocally unjust. He'd threatened my life. He'd force-fed me my own feces. He'd conspired to desecrate my body and humiliate me by baiting me with false hope. Shaming him for those actions was no equal crime. But if I refused to atone for turning the world against him, he very well might just kill me.

Honestly, what choice would he have? He'd *have to* kill me. If not, he might do something even *more* heinous. Something only he could dream up.

Either way, I wanted to puke.

This obsessive panic wore me thin before supper, so I left my phone in my room, alerts all set to silent. At the table, we all talked about what an accomplishment it was for Mr. Branch to finally fix the air conditioning unit without professional guidance, the proper tools, or a high school diploma. He praised the beauty of the internet and, specifically, YouTube tutorials. It felt nice to exist in a world where small talk mattered, even if just for a moment. We were just three people in a room, talking while we ate. It felt sacred.

The room cooled as we ate, and an appreciation sprouted for the man who'd made it happen. Not unlike the internet, Mr. Branch was mostly foul—by any standard, but speckled with brilliant flashes of humanity. I watched his weathered eyes as he looked down at his plate, and I resisted the urge to wrap my arms around him and say I was sorry. Or maybe just call him *Pops* again.

We put our dishes in the sink, and I hesitated before retreating to my room. Maybe I wanted to volunteer to help with the dishes—a first in my lifetime—or maybe I just couldn't face what that little black screen might reveal when I unlocked it. I turned around and watched my folks cleaning up, trying to think of something to say, until they both looked up at me. I smiled at Dad and gave a thumbs-up.

"Thanks for getting the air going again, Pops. It feels amazing."

He replied with a single nod, bunching his lips together before turning away. I proceeded to my room and closed the door. Before I made it to the bed, I decided to open it again. I'd gotten so used to life without that cool comfort, I forgot I had to let it in.

AS ANTICIPATED, MY PHONE WAS ALIGHT WITH NOTIFICATIONS. The only way to go through them without overwhelming myself would be to establish a hierarchy of importance. Calls, voicemails, and texts would have to be at the top, since they'd be from those who had my phone number—whether I knew the people or not, they were a top concern. The next tier down would be emails and direct messages. Email was important for academic purposes, and direct messages were usually juicy. It might be silly to put these on an equal plane, but it made sense to me. Last would be social media alerts—now the most daunting workload of all, and one I avoided.

The first texts (aside from group conversations, which I hated and never checked) were from Seth, who sent me screenshots of the numbers below my social media posts, and shamelessly reminded me that he'd been my friend when no one else was willing to be. He even went so far as to minimize the value of Ray Mack's friendship, citing his fair-weather allegiance and rubbery backbone.

I chuckled upon seeing the next set of text messages from Ray, and sought to reaffirm our friendship. His unsolicited, chummy tone sounded so uncharacteristic that I wondered if he outsourced those messages to someone with more proficient social skills. I only thought better of it because I knew he was an only child with no friends, and no money to hire someone.

The last message made my breathing hitch. It was from Trinity.

> Guess u cant take a joke, fucking incel… touch my brother again and see what happens u fat queer

The *nerve* of this bitch. I seethed, trying to think up the harshest reply I could, when Dad startled me with a forced cough as he leaned on the doorjamb, eyes downturned and hands in his pockets. I sat up, greeting him with the obligatory "Hey."

"I gotta head out for work a couple hours early tonight," he said. "We got a, uh, special order shipment coming in 'cause of the wildfires out west messing up the supply chain. I can't very well call mandatory overtime for the shift and not be there myself, ya know?" He let out an unsmiling chortle.

"Oh, alright then," I said. "I was probably gonna hit the hay soon, anyway. School and all that's got me pretty wore out."

"Course." He nudged himself off the doorjamb, but I could tell he had more to say. After an agonizing silence and two failed attempts to look me in the eyes, he sucked his teeth and drummed his hands on his jeans. "Listen, ah—I just wanted to let you know, ah . . . you know, I uh—well, sometimes I say what I'm thinking without really thinking about it, if that makes any sense."

"I know, Pops."

His voice had a faint quiver. "But no matter what I say, or what anyone else says . . . you're my boy, alright?" He choked up and abruptly disappeared down the hall.

I had to say something, but what came out even caught me by surprise. "I love you, too!"

He didn't respond, but I knew he heard me. I just wondered

if he picked up on the tremors in my own voice when I said it. Part of me hoped he did.

I wasn't sure if Mom was still home or not, so I got up and locked my door shut. My room hadn't cooled as much as I'd have liked, but the privacy to break down uninterrupted was more important. I knelt at my bedside and buried my face in the pillow with the same calm urgency as if I needed to purge my stomach contents into the toilet. Once the new chairman in headquarters gave the signal, the floodgates opened. I vomited my hard feelings until my temples bulged. Much like puking, there was no stopping once it started.

Crying sucked. I *reviled* it. Aside from running, it might've been my least favorite thing to do. People probably assumed someone like me cried a lot, but I didn't. It'd always felt dangerous to me. If I started crying, why would I ever stop? My life, my size, my appearance—none of it was going to change, so what good would it do to cry about it? In my mind, nothing could be sadder than a fat guy sobbing, and I refused to be a sad case. If I got used to it, what would stop me from letting the assholes of the world catch me in the act? That alone was a risk I couldn't afford. With so many other coping mechanisms at my disposal, it'd become a last resort. *Dead* last.

Of course, there's a glaring problem with this approach. I had plenty to cry about, overweight or not. Years of feeling unloved by the only two people I loved left a hole that couldn't be filled, no matter the level of success I achieved in online role-playing games, or how delicious the food I stuffed down my gullet was. I'd never been in denial of this, but I wouldn't have to be if I never admitted such a void existed in the first place.

Just as I'd feared over the decade or so since I'd last wept, it felt *amazing*. The years of pent-up emotional toxicity poured out into that pillow, and the supply seemed abundant. It got to the point where I fed it, conjuring up images that tore my insides apart—Dad fighting tears, the kids in every classroom from kindergarten through junior year laughing at my expense, and Trinity's taunting pretty face, deliberately baiting me with the false hope that I might not be repugnant—at least, not to *everyone*. One by one, I piled on new pains and insecurities like fresh logs tossed onto a burgeoning campfire.

This episode lasted into the night, until the tears literally ran dry. I still cried, but no moisture ran from my eyes. I stopped being able to breathe through my nose, and my head started pounding, so I made an effort to end the spell. My eyelids had swollen so heavy and puffy I had to strain to keep them open. At some point, as I lay on my bed, I quit straining. And they stayed closed.

I WOKE UP FULLY DRESSED AND DRENCHED IN SWEAT, MY EYES crusted shut. Mom pounded on my door, her frenetic yelling indiscernible. I shouted something to indicate I was okay, and that I'd come out in a bit. Whatever I said worked, granting me a few minutes of silence to process yet another time warp. I grabbed my phone to check the time, only to find it dead. Plugging it in revealed another barrage of notifications I struggled to sort out. But more daunting than that was the time displayed at the top-right: *8:07 a.m.*

Shit. I'd missed the bus.

My clothes were soaked in sweat, so before anything else, I changed. I went into the bathroom as Mom yelled from the living room—something about driving me to school. The mirror showed me a face that had no business going to school, or being seen by anyone, for that matter. My eyes were so puffy and red that they looked diseased. Dried snot encrusted the peach fuzz hairs on my upper lip. I peed for a duration that had to be a personal record, cleaned up a bit, then went out to face Mom.

I walked into the living room. "Ma, I can't go to school today."

She scoffed without looking up from her phone. "The hell you can't!"

"Look at me, Ma."

She did. Her mouth fell open. "Oh my lord, son! What the hell's happened to you? Is that an allergic reaction? Did something bite you?" She got up and shuffled over to me to investigate closer.

I held my hands up. "Naw, Ma. I'm just—I need a mental health day, or whatever."

Her face twisted in a sour frown. "*Mental health day?* The hell does that mean? What's happened to your eyes?"

My shoulders slumped as I realized I'd have to spell it out for her. "I've been *crying*, Ma." (I whispered the word *crying* the same way she and Dad whispered *Black people* when there might be Black people around.)

"Aw, honey! Are you alright? What's got you so upset, baby boy?" Her expression softened as she reached up to brush my cheek.

I flinched, recoiling from her touch. "Yeah, I'm alright. I just need a day to get my head right, is all. I won't be missing anything important this early in the year. Second day of the year, they're still telling us the rules and such."

Her face bent in a cynical frown. "You're not staying home to play video games all day, now."

I raised my right hand and shook my head. "I won't. No games at all. Promise."

With that, she relented, and I had the day to slow time down to a manageable pace. She made breakfast and pried for more details, which I easily sidestepped. As we ate, I threw her a bone by divulging the full exchange between me and Dad, where he'd suggested I might not be his. She became agitated, swearing him off and promising he had no reason to suspect her infidelity. Apparently, they'd fought over the topic after I left for the first day of school, and she rehashed what was said between them. As the conversation turned into a Dad-bashing session, I relayed the gist of his exchange with me the night before, in which he reaffirmed his role as my father. I made her promise not to tell him I told her, then retreated to my room for a day of sorting out my chaotic new viral existence.

In accordance with the hierarchy of notifications, I checked my text messages first. This time, I sorted those in their own scaffold of importance, by individual sender (as per usual, I ignored all group conversations). The first was from Trinity.

> Ppl are sending chip death threats thanks to you. I hope ur happy u fat fuking faggo

I hoped that was a lie, for my own sake alone. My first thought was that I was glad I didn't respond to her text from yesterday, in case someone actually killed him and I incriminated myself. I'd had every intention of doubling down on what I'd done to cast a light on his behavior. My next thought was that there was no way the people of the internet were that fanatical. Why would anyone be so affected by a stranger's experience to send death threats to their tormentor? If I didn't feel the need to threaten his life, why should anyone else? I doubted her claim and moved on to the next messages in the pecking order, which came from Seth.

I scrolled past the several screenshots substantiating my stardom, until I landed on his litany of texts.

> I heard they gonna talk about you on Jimmy Kimmel tonight u lucky asshole
>
> Damn u ugly as shit wit no clothes on bro lololol wtf did you drink to pass out naked like that lol
>
> U didn't really eat shit tho, right? U made that up lol
>
> Ain't no way that little fucker made u eat shit [cry-

laugh emoji]

Yo are you even alive bro? Why ain't you at shool?

Only then did it register—my now famous content included me accusing Chip of feeding me shit. In the moment, I'd felt no shame about this because my only emotion was rage. But now, it seemed like that whole encounter had been a movie. And the video Trinity posted of my nude body was now public domain. I cringed so hard it required both hands to rub my forehead.

Why did I do this to myself? I thought. *What the hell was I thinking?*

After a minute or so regretting my life choices, I picked up my phone and got back to work. The next unread text was from an unknown number.

U win, lard ass. Can't wait till I see u again lol

Now, don't get me wrong. Plenty of people had called me *lard ass* over the years. But until that text, I hadn't realized how dated the term had become. I couldn't recall anyone firing that insult at me since at least middle school. It's almost as if it'd been retired from the lineup, and by some unofficial decree, the assholes at school all agreed to stop using it.

Except one.

Chip hurled so many nasty things my way over the course of one year that he had to dig deep in his bag to keep the insults fresh. And *lard ass* was one of them. It had to be him who'd sent that text. If not, then I didn't care.

But if so, what did he mean? I . . . *win?* What, was he surrendering? It certainly didn't give me that vibe, considering he punctuated it with a veiled threat. What was he going to do when he saw me again? If he planned on killing me, he obviously didn't plan on getting away with it. Once again, I considered bringing my concerns to the authorities. I could only hope they wouldn't be so naïve to take his *lol* seriously.

I'd have to mull it over, I figured. And before I did anything, I had to sift through all this internet fame to see just how much I'd blown up. Seth regurgitated the hearsay that I'd get a mention on a nationally televised late-night talk show, which sounded like bullshit, so I had to get an accurate reading.

Based on what I found on social media, his claims were plausible. Accurate, even. I had over three hundred direct messages on Instagram, and tens of thousands of likes on each of my posts. Even my TikTok account had blown up, boasting a following of over two hundred thousand, despite no engagement from me. Candace's video on Instagram had a view count in the tens of millions, and hundreds of thousands of likes and comments. I read a few comments, and the top ones applauded me for standing up to my bully. But further down the line, they got nastier. Most people had fat jokes—some of which I had to admit were funny—and derision at my overall appearance. You know, the underbelly of mankind's collective consciousness.

My own posts had a similar makeup, but with testimonials by other overweight people who sympathized with my struggle. Many of them had advice on how to lose weight, ranging from juice cleanses to thirty-day challenges, to crystals, to gastric bypass surgery. Others just thanked me for sharing my story. I spent what turned out to be hours on end looking through the best of these comments, learning quickly how to filter out the ones that pissed me off.

The direct messages were much more heartening. The vast majority were sent by people dealing with obesity who wanted to share their own experiences and thank me for validating them. I read each and every one, even replying to some when they hit me hard enough. I found these anecdotes to be a welcome side effect to the less-than-desirable desired effects of my online fame. I never wanted to be a star; I just wanted to live my life without harassment. Going viral was no way to accomplish what I really wanted.

I stared blankly at my phone's lock screen. Then it hit me. This was never supposed to be about me, and those messages reminded me of that.

B Y THE TIME I'D FINISHED PORING OVER MY INSTAGRAM AND
TikTok notifications, it was midafternoon. I left my phone
in my room, as though it was my nagging job. I watched mindless
daytime TV until Dad arose for his breakfast, which was our
supper. Spirits among us Branches were higher than ever, and
we all convened to enjoy my favorite meal—Ma's lasagna—over
a jovial conversation.

For the most part, we discussed the craziness Dad dealt with
at work, and I had no desire to change the subject. He talked
about the work they did with their hands and machines, and how
their paper and cardboard products were in high demand due to
a diminishing supply. His crew pulled long hours, missing time
with their families to get their jobs done, and all for the benefit
of consumers somewhere down the line who'd never know the
sacrifices made for them. Sure, those workers actually did it for
the overtime pay, under the threat of losing their livelihoods,
but the end result was a benefit to society. I could see how tired
Dad was, and I appreciated everything he did for us. *Why* he
was tired.

What charmed me most about his account of his workday
was the fact that it somehow dwarfed my global fame. He hadn't
heard a word about me becoming an internet star, because it

didn't really matter. No one would lose their jobs, their resources, or their purpose in life because they hadn't reaped the benefits of my so-called product. Everything that'd concerned me over the last few days lacked substance, and this realization was as refreshing as the cool air now sucking the heat off the back of my neck.

After supper, Dad sprawled on the couch, nestling his head into the cushion the way he would when preparing for a nap. It was seven at night, which was an unusual time for him to do so. I couldn't recall the last work night he'd taken a nap after supper.

I cocked my head and flashed him a playful frown. "Getting a little siesta before your shift, huh?"

"Boy, you know damn well it's Friday. Now don't you wake me 'til Sunday."

It's Friday?

I did the math in my head, and it checked out. With the first day of school landing mid-week, and time flying by at a breakneck pace, I'd lost track of the week. Throughout my imaginary headquarters, intercoms played the crescendo of Beethoven's *Ode to Joy*, and the guys in my head plopped back in their chairs, exhausted and elated. With a jubilant salutation for the folks, I retired to my room to waste away another forty-eight hours.

The *World of Warcraft* awaited me, and I obliged. My phone lay dying on the bed while I took a break from being Fat Chance of the Internet and became the relatively anonymous user *take_a_chnce*. I slayed fictional, non-player beasts and other users alike, leading my group with fearless abandon. My adventures ended in the small hours of the night, and I relished the unimportance of what I'd done with my time.

Funny how those meaningless moments can mean so much.

I did very much the same with my Saturday, only taking breaks for bathroom, meals, mandated chores, and essential hygiene. I left my phone dormant on the nightstand, a relic of an intentionally forgotten existence. Also reminiscent of the ancient past, I didn't even bring it with me to take a dump, instead reading Tolkien or graphic novels—hard copies, on glossed paper.

I'd learned the truth, which could never be unlearned. Nothing in that little rectangular device could possibly bring me joy, despite the fervor with which it promised to do exactly that.

Only later would I learn that this is a brilliant strategy to increase online traction. By neglecting to acknowledge any of the comments and (most of) the direct messages, I fostered the illusion that I'd "been there before" and was thereby aloof, thus perpetuating my *above-it-all* persona. In my deliberate negligence, I'd behaved like a celebrity, which led to my becoming even more celebrated.

Sunday night, I ended my procrastination and checked my socials. Instagram, TikTok, Snapchat, and even the boomer platforms—Twitter and Facebook—still showed flourishing numbers. Email proved especially daunting since I hadn't checked it all week. To my relief, Jimmy Kimmel had not requested my presence on his show. I plowed through the notifications, clearing them unless they were direct messages from Candace, texts from saved numbers, or anything else I felt deserved my immediate attention, such as academic alerts.

I prepared to toss the phone aside when, on a whim, I decided to see how Chip and Trinity were holding up through all of this. If it was this exhausting being the hero in the public narrative, I could only imagine what the villains were going through—not that I pitied them in the least.

Chip's Instagram had disappeared, which meant he'd either deleted his profile or blocked me. He didn't have any other socials I could find, except a dormant Facebook profile with nothing but a grainy family photo featuring a much younger him. Trinity hadn't posted anything new, and all the pictures and videos she'd posted before I went viral had been taken down.

So essentially, nothing.

But just before I locked my phone screen, the count of unread text messages caught my eye. Instead of an actual number, the little red bubble just indicated *999+*. It piqued my curiosity, so I investigated.

The group chats I'd been ignoring made up the bulk of that count—of which there were five. I went to the one with the most unread messages, and it had thirty-one other contacts in the conversation. I scrolled up, reading the discussion in reverse, trying to make sense of it. All I could tell was that it was vitriolic, but lacked specifics. Frustrated, I flung my thumb up the screen to scroll back by a matter of days, finally halting the search when the term *death threats* caught my eye.

> I heard he got death threats from someone from school
>
> It wasn't me lol… but if he dies its whatever

They had to be talking about Chip. I dug deeper to catch up on what they'd been saying the last few days.

The reason I hated group text conversations so much is because they were *work*. If I wasn't willing to spend my valued time reading the whining narration of Holden Caulfield in exchange for a decent grade, why would I treat the typo-riddled blasé streams of consciousness spouted by my idiot classmates in return for *nothing?* No thanks, I'll get the CliffsNotes. It didn't help that the topic of conversation was usually sports, relationships, or dances, or some gossip about other kids I didn't care about. And that's if everyone wasn't talking shit about me in particular. For me, there'd never been motivation to read that drivel.

But even now, as I knew I rose in popularity at Chandler's Marsh High School, their words still offered little upside for me. Were they saying I'm great, now that I'm famous? If so, then as far as I care, they can all do just as I'd done, and *eat my shit.*

This attitude toward group texts worked just fine for me, as I saw it. I'd never regret not knowing what was being said—except now. I didn't care what everyone said about *me*—the object of my concern was Chip. I needed to know what they were saying about him, although I hadn't quite pinpointed why.

I gathered the gist of their rancor. Without me as their punching bag, they needed a new one, and Chip was their huckleberry. Apparently, he'd sat alone at lunch on Friday and had a large gash on the side of his face. Even Todd Simpson turned against him, saying Chip had forced him to cooperate in the setup to humiliate me under the threat of badgering Todd's mom at the IHOP where she served. (I wasn't sure I believed that, but I also wasn't sure whether I wanted to or not.)

The big rumor going around school was that Trinity was supposed to have been a senior last year, but she dropped out of school to become a prostitute before the Smiths moved to town. That buzz was substantiated by the supposedly verified fact that their dad, Roscoe, was unemployed and trying to pay the bills as a freelance landscaper—thereby debunking their claim that they'd moved to Chandler's Marsh at his employer's behest. *Of course,* I thought, scoffing. *The first time my lips touched a girl's, she was a hooker.* While I'd always expected as much, I always thought it would've happened later in life, and that I'd pay for it with earned money; not my widespread humiliation.

Another noteworthy tidbit I picked up regarded their mother. Supposedly, Trinity turned to prostitution to pay the rent because their mother had been the primary breadwinner until she was killed by a drunk driver. The text participants speculated wildly about this, but there seemed to be veracity to this manner of death—I checked it out on the web. The conjecture ran amok about why the family would go broke as a result, given that drunk driving deaths usually carried some kind of monetary settlement. I tried to interpret anything coherent in their guesswork, but it all made as much sense as particle physics—albeit on the other end of the intellectual spectrum.

The rest of the text conversation was arduous, except for a few funny memes and GIFs. I got tired of everyone piling on Chip just because I'd made it the cool thing to do. If I'd kept my phone in my pocket that first day of school, they'd probably be trashing me instead. I locked my phone without bothering to go through the other group chats. The stupidity I witnessed in one thread was enough to make my eyes cross. Maybe I'd peruse them some other day, when things got boring again.

As I lay in bed, daydreaming about living in a cabin deep in the woods with high-speed internet access—as I often did when it was time to turn my brain off—my thoughts wandered. The guys in my brain sat around the long table in their conference room, debating whether or not I should have sympathy for Chip Smith. Those in favor were obviously in the minority, but made a compelling case.

Without excusing his transgressions, I understood how it felt to be in everyone's crosshairs. Did he deserve it? Hell yes, he did. But that didn't change the fact that I felt bad for him. If I could just get an apology out of him, I could probably call off the angry mob, and help him down from the gallows. The truth was that I didn't hate my ongoing abuse by society just because it happened *to me*. I hated that it happened *at all*.

The majority of the guys in my head couldn't deny this, as little as they wanted to hear it. Their point, which resonated louder than the dissenters due to their numbers alone, was that my very humanity had been undermined. All I'd done to Chip—aside from choking him out against the lockers—was show the world his true character. Whatever consequences he reaped now were a product of the behavior he'd sown, and that was none of my concern. I had good reason to wish for a return to obscurity, and my conscience should bear none of the burden for his offenses.

Although there was a consensus in that deliberation, one of those guys must've had veto power. I decided—if for no other reason than the need for sleep—that I had to at least grant Chip the opportunity to apologize. I knew if he had remorse, it would change my thinking. It would soften me. I couldn't in good conscience slap a contrite hand away, and I understood this about myself. If he passed up that opportunity, I'd stay the course and crush him; but I had to commit to a good-faith effort if I wanted a restful night's sleep.

By Sunday morning, my anxious thoughts shifted to the actual schooling part of school, and the work I'd missed. I realized I'd never checked PowerSchool—the online assignment board—or caught up on anything I'd missed on Friday. Upon doing so, I came to terms with starting the year behind the curve and debated whether I should scramble and grovel to catch up, or just be cool with a C average again. This was a no-brainer, in the end, considering how little I could move the needle on my GPA after three full years of mediocre grades.

On Monday, one of the special kids on the bus approached me for an autograph, which caught me by surprise. All I could do was frown and say no. I didn't want to be mean, but the absurdity of it soured my mood. *Why the hell would you want my autograph, you dumbshit?* I thought all the way to school. *Do you think it's gonna be worth money someday?* I'm sure I came off like a self-important asshole, but it was the exact opposite. Autographs are supposed to be from people who've done something extraordinary. Not *me*. Perhaps I overreacted, but I preferred that to being the vain asshole who signed an autograph for an intellectually disabled kid boarding the short bus, just because I'd become a fleeting internet star for a few dumb videos.

There was no mob waiting in the unloading area this time, but a few underclassmen did point as I emerged from the bus. I could feel a few bystanders recording as I walked the halls, probably vying for their own piece of the internet stardom pie. Seth greeted me at my homeroom door, espousing my growing brand. He pitched the idea of Fat Chance T-shirts and hoodies on the way to my seat, going into the numbers he'd crunched until the teacher told him to go to his assigned seat. When the first-period bell rang, he picked up where he'd left off, following me to my locker and pointing to his open notebook full of circled numbers and arrows.

As I looked him in the face to tell him to chill on the business idea, I caught sight of a face in the passing crowd. Chip Smith, walking all alone, his expression stoic as a mannequin's. The left side of his face—the spot where I'd called him out for wearing concealer—boasted a harsh, pink abrasion. He walked right by me, but kept his eyes fixed straight ahead, as though he didn't see me. If I weren't me, I might assume he hadn't noticed my presence, but I could safely take his lack of acknowledgment as an icy gesture.

I would've felt better if he'd said anything at all.

Math and history were uneventful, aside from the endless glances in my direction and whatever the course material was. Kids whispered to each other, and like always, I knew it was about me—but this time it didn't sting as much as it annoyed me. I sat up a little straighter knowing I was the most famous kid in the room, no matter what room I was in.

The attention increased as the day went on, and by lunchtime, I was ready to hop on top of a table and tell the entire student body to kiss my fat ass. They'd treated me like a freak my entire life, and now they gawked at me like some sort of celebrity, just for putting this shithole town on the map.

Seth and Ray joined me in the lunch line and followed me to my table like hired goons. All the while, Seth beleaguered the business venture idea to the point where Ray and I exchanged glances of exasperation, and tried at every opportunity to change the subject. It was Mexican pizza day, so I tuned him out and focused on the joyous Mariachi band playing on my tongue rather than listening to Seth's overbearing salesmanship.

If anything might shut him up, it'd be the presence of a female—and she appeared, godsend that she was. Candace stopped behind Seth, smiling at me with her lunch tray in hand.

"Hey Chance," she said. Her brown eyes looked right at me, and I couldn't control the look on my face.

I finished chewing my mouthful of Americanized ethnic pizza. "Hey, Candace. How's it going?"

"Not too bad," she said, flashing her eyebrows. "I gotta say, I owe you one. My following is like, quadruple what it was. Maybe more. I even have advertisers now. You put on quite a show!"

I shrugged humbly. "I give the commoners what they want," I said.

I'll never know what made me say that, but her reaction will stick with me forever. She blurted a laugh loud enough to echo off the cafeteria walls, drawing the attention of everyone near us. She covered her mouth, and her face reddened, as though she should be embarrassed.

"Spoken like a true noble," she said. She tucked a tendril of hair behind one ear and smiled. "Whenever you get around to my text . . . I'm still waiting for an answer."

My jaw dropped, and I retrieved my phone. "What text?" But just as I said that, I found the unread message.

> Sooo my royal subjects are clamoring for your presence on the court… in case you didn't know, I'm a queen lol. Anyway, there's a renaissance festival up in Kingdom City in a couple weeks… do you want to join us? We have a van rented

I tried to play it cool, I really did. But even in the moment, I could feel my face growing pink and my mouth going dry. I smacked my tongue and met her gaze. "I'd love to."

She giggled and looked at her feet, then looked me in the eye. "You won't be disappointed. These people worshiped you even before some dork created the Fat Chance hashtag."

We both laughed, and she departed with a flirtatious wave before returning her attention to her phone. Seth raved about how uncontrollably attracted to me she was, and all the things she wanted to do to me, but his words landed on my ears like white noise. Ray watched her walk away and commented on how he'd always liked her, further inflating my already floating head.

How many years had it been? Ten? Twelve? I'd known Candace longer than most of my extended family—well, known *of* her, anyway. All that time, we'd never had a real conversation— mostly because I'd freeze up or reply monosyllabically when she talked to me. Now, in front of my only two friends, she'd said more to me within one minute than in all the years before. My heart leapt in my chest, begging to follow her for more of this feeling. I watched her walk away, admiring the way her clothes draped over her plump body, accentuating every curve. It wasn't until she took her seat and looked back at me that I realized I'd been staring. My head snapped down to my tray, and I let my thoughts wander. I went into my phone to admire her text one more time, but found she'd sent me another just seconds ago.

Btw you can call me Candy… but only in private lol

Saccharine '80s rock ballads serenaded me in my head, even though I didn't actually know the songs. It was some mixture of Journey and REO Speedwagon, or whatever other bands my dad always raved about. My heart swelled, and I realized the feelings I'd had for Trinity were far too small to have affected me the way they did. Candace—or should I say, *Candy*—could *really* hurt me if she wanted to, with my soul now resting firmly in her grasp. For someone like me, the least bit of emotional vulnerability can become catastrophic.

We finished eating, not without Seth's spirited blathering about my budding affection for Candace, and how she and I would be the emperors of the apparel company he was going to help us create. Ray went silent, stealing glances in her direction every chance he got. I stood, shamelessly excusing myself to—as I so put it so chivalrously—"bombard the porcelain fortifications with mine army's armament."

It was the most refined manner in which I'd ever excused myself to pinch a loaf in my entire life, and I chuckled at it on the walk down the hall. I may as well have become a dirigible—my feet didn't seem to touch the ground. My viral fame mattered even less than it had at the start of this day, except for it putting me in conversational contact with Candy Klauss. I tried my best not to look like I skipped down the hallway with glee, but I have to believe my gait betrayed me. I took a deep breath and turned into the boys' bathroom.

Unlike any time before, I stopped before ducking into a stall to take a look at myself in the mirror. I bared my teeth, reassuring myself I hadn't had a speck of chili pepper lodged between any of them during my exchange with her. With another heavy sigh, I turned around to tend to the business at hand.

My favorite stall door clunked open. Someone was already in there. Before I could cast my eyes away courteously as the occupant emerged, I saw his face.

Chip.

23

H E LEERED AT ME WITH AN EXPRESSION I COULDN'T IDENTIFY. I froze. Unsure what else to do as he looked at me from beneath his eyebrows, I said the first thing that came to mind.

"Hey, Chip." I tilted my head back and looked down my nose, flaunting my dignity. An apology might come, and I'd wait for it, awkward as the silence might be. I'd resolved to give him a chance, so I locked eyes with him as he took a straddled stance in front of me.

He shrugged. "Looks like you win, *Fat Chance.*"

I snorted. "*Win?*"

Tears filled his eyes as he muscled a grin, then he scowled. "You got what you wanted, didn't ya? It's me against the whole world now. That's what you wanted."

"I don't think you know what I want."

"You know, it's true what they're saying," he said, ignoring me. "My momma got killed by a drunk driver. And we didn't get no money from it. Know why that is?"

I shook my head slowly.

"The drunk driver," he said, sputtering a laugh, "was my piece of shit daddy." His laugh twisted into a crying frown.

I slumped. "Oh my God. I'm sorry, Chip."

"Yeah, ya are." A tear streaked down one cheek.

I had a chance to say something there, but I hesitated. What could I possibly say? I searched for the right words but came up empty. Consoling others was a foreign skill to me, since I was typically the saddest person in the room.

If there's one true regret in my life, it's my failure to be a good human in that moment. To say something better than whatever the next dumbass would say in that situation. Chip was hurting, and like a cornered animal, he lashed out at the nearest threat to forestall his own vulnerability. I took another deep breath and said the only thing that came to mind.

"Are *you?*"

His eyes disappeared in a hateful squint, and he stepped toward me. "What, you want an apology, fat boy? 'Cause you're gonna be wantin' a long time. I ain't sorry for *shit*, you fat fuck. You think you're better than me all a sudden, but you're still that disgusting blob that passed out naked on my sister's bed, ya tiny pecker motherfucker. Always will be. Won't ya?"

I shrugged. His disappointment in this reaction showed.

He lifted his black *Tapout* T-shirt and drew the .44 Magnum that'd so often appeared in my nightmares. He grabbed it by the barrel and flicked the ivory handle in front of my face. "Take it," he said, his voice trembling. "And put a bullet in my head. I *do* know what you want. It's exactly that. So, go on—take it."

My jaw clenched. I shook my head and tried to say no.

"You said you're sorry, didn't ya? Well, if you're sorry for me, then put an end to it. Go on!" He slapped my chest with the gun's grip, then waved it in front of my nose. "Put me down like a wounded dog! If you got mercy for me, then end it!" His eyes welled full of tears.

"Chip . . ." I took the kindest tone I could muster. "I forgive you."

His eyes flickered wide, like he'd been shocked with a thousand volts. He grabbed the gun's grip with the other hand. As he squeezed his eyes shut, tears streamed out from the corners. The big gun's muzzle pushed hard underneath his jaw.

I'd never forget the little whimper he let out before he pulled the trigger.

The sound hurt my ears. I must've blinked from the flash, because all I remember after the bang was him being gone from sight. He was there, and then . . . he wasn't. For whatever reason, my first reaction was to look up. A fine red spray painted the ceiling, with a dark hole at the center. I swallowed hard, and tasted a trace of iron. I looked down at Chip Smith's lifeless body. A crimson pool grew around what remained of his head, like a morbid halo. His body lay in a contorted position comfortable only for the dead.

A ringing deafened me, then blended into a high-pitched wail I soon realized was my own voice. I babbled incoherently as a couple teachers and a student ran into the restroom. Only when they neared me did I realize I was on my knees and teetering over. I tried to steady myself on the sink counter, but slipped.

I'd lost consciousness before, but this time was different. The dreams I had were so surreal, but yet so believable that I remember thinking reality was the nightmare, and I hadn't seen what I thought I'd seen. In this alternate universe, some other worrisome thing happened to me, erasing any trace of seeing my bully blow his head off. The frenzied sounds echoing in the bathroom lured me back to the forgotten real world, seemingly weeks after I'd left it.

24

I NEVER FOUND OUT WHETHER I HIT MY HEAD OR JUST PASSED out from shock, but I awoke to Mr. Dorchester holding my head up and fanning me. The scene around me set in. I looked down at my body, and my shirt was stained with a dark red mist that grew denser as it neared my face. The bloody flavor lingered in my mouth. I tried to speak, but Mr. Dorchester and the guidance counselor kept interrupting, imploring me to focus on breathing.

The flurry of activity around me added to the surrealism. I moved in slow motion while the world around me scurried to call for help, hold the gawking students back, and get me up off the floor. Three teachers guarded the body, standing shoulder to shoulder to shield my eyes. I didn't want to see it again, but my eyes gravitated to it involuntarily. Through all the obstacles, I caught one last glimpse of the body that used to be Chip, and the image will stick with me until my dying day.

This asshole who'd tormented me so badly—the personification of the world's disdain for me—no longer had a recognizable head. The brain responsible for all the plots to terrorize, humiliate, and dehumanize me no longer resided in his skull. The face I loathed for a full year had become an unrecognizable red mass.

I rose to my feet and leaned on the counter until my heart pumped enough blood to my brain to keep from fainting again. Mr. Dorchester and Mr. Nagy escorted me by the elbows, doing their best to steady me as I walked out of that unholy bathroom—although all they really did was make me worry I'd crush one of them if I tipped over again. My ears whooshed in a cyclical pattern with each heartbeat, and I promised myself I wouldn't die of a heart attack right then. Not at school. Not with Chip still in the room, his brains looking down on me. No—I'd at least make it home and have a coronary, stroke, or aneurysm in my own bed. But every hard rush of blood through my ears felt like it might be the last.

In the hallway, everyone crowded behind an invisible barrier created by the school resource officer's outstretched arms. The principal looked over everyone's heads and made some sort of announcement I couldn't hear. The outer limits of my vision closed in, slowly stealing my vision away. I heard the clang of my head against the lockers, and the next thing I knew, I lay on a stretcher as a team of EMTs heaved me into the back of an ambulance.

They took me to the hospital as a precaution since it was the second time I'd lost consciousness in less than five minutes, and I'd hit my head pretty hard on the way down. It also helped that the paramedics were there just in case Chip had clung to life, but had nothing better to do upon their arrival—only the coroner would tend to him. Mom and Dad showed up and greeted me with the most profuse and unbridled display of affection I'd ever seen. The way they acted, I thought they misunderstood what'd happened. I actually told my mom I hadn't been shot as she buried her face in my chest and sobbed.

Turns out, while I hadn't had a heart attack or stroke,

my blood pressure was sky high—the upper end of stage two hypertension. Off the chart, even for someone my size, and even for someone who'd just witnessed a gruesome suicide.

The numbers were so grave, they admitted me in pretty short order. In yet another blur, I went from the mayhem at the school to the tranquility of a cushy hospital room. My folks had to wait a while to join me in the room, so I lay in the bed alone, staring at a manufactured watercolor on the wall, wondering how I'd ever recover from this. I'd like to say I found some kind of simplistic wisdom in the depiction of a grey sky over a rural field painted yellow by dandelions, but the cheap artwork was merely a point on which to fix my eyes.

The attending doctor ran a battery of tests, but couldn't come to a definitive conclusion until he asked if I had any trouble breathing. That's when Mom volunteered the anecdote about thinking I was dead that one morning. This was the missing piece of the puzzle, apparently. The doc said sleep apnea causes hypertension, acid reflux (which I'd always attributed to my weight), and can shave upwards of fifteen years off of life expectancy. In tandem with my obesity and sedentary lifestyle, the doctor warned my parents they might bury me if something didn't change.

The first of the changes to come was the CPAP machine, which turned sleeping—one of my favorite activities—into a scuba diving exercise. Every night, presumably for the rest of my life, I'd strap a breathing apparatus onto my face and drift into slumber to the tune of a white noise hiss. The first few times, I found it impossible to ignore the intrusive hoses and sounds. But soon enough, I learned to fantasize I was an astronaut rigged for travel through deep space, and the apparatus was there to ensure I stayed alive through the years of stasis. Call it silly, but it worked. My best friend had always been my imagination.

Grief counseling was offered to everyone at school, but very few families in our staunchly rural community believed in such sorcery outside of the church. My doctor suggested counseling for me with a bit more insistence than a standing offer. I believe the term he used was *medical necessity*. Dad was not only resistant to clinical therapy, but diametrically opposed to it. Part of me wondered if he thought talking to someone with letters behind their name might turn me into a vegan, homosexual, or liberal—or the dreaded combination of all three. I had to admire the doctor's patience and decorum, given the way my father berated him. In the end, he was able to convince my dad I'd live with post-traumatic stress for the remainder of my days, and my quality of life would depend almost entirely on how well I learned to manage it.

Mom, on the other hand, embraced it. Over the years, she'd been the only emotional support in our single-wide trailer. Granted, she sucked at it, but she was better than nothing. The reality of what I'd seen and the damage it'd done to me struck her in the mother bone hidden somewhere deep within her. She took me to all my appointments. On the way there, she'd urge me to be honest with the therapist, and that it was okay to cry if I needed to. On the way back, she'd ask how it went, and pry for more details than HIPAA would view as compliant with medical privacy laws.

I suppose my discretion in telling her most of what I talked about in the sessions served the greater good, though. My growth in the process of self-examination prompted Mom to seek out a support group for her own psychological ills. Only then did I come to learn that she had a gambling addiction. It made so many pieces fit. The money disappearing, the weird chunks of time she was gone—disillusioning as it was, I was so relieved to know she was playing bingo and betting on horses, and not prostituting herself for a fix of meth.

None of this is meant to paint a rosy picture of my psychological recovery. It was miserable. My shrink, Erin, softened the blow with her delicate demeanor. She had this charismatic technique where I didn't even notice I was opening up to her. After a half hour of what felt like unguided bullshitting, I'd be ugly-crying like the fat baby I came into the world as.

Therapy sessions felt like picking mental scabs—how would I ever get past this traumatic event if we just kept rehashing it all the time? Why is it so important that I cry? Why must every emotion be measured on a scale from one to ten? Of course, I'd later understand the answers to these rhetorical questions, but it was hard to trust the process in the moment. If Erin hadn't been so endearing, I might've quit going, strangled her, or embraced my downward spiral, because the cure often felt worse than the disease.

My inability to eat anything red and liquidy anymore—which included my favorite dessert, strawberry shortcake—was bad enough. Between that and my aversion to anything brown or mushy, all the favorite things in my diet were disappearing because of my traumas.

But so were my favorite activities—namely, my very favorite: sleeping. I couldn't sleep without nightmares, and I began to experience a terrifying phenomenon. *Sleep paralysis.* I'd wake up in the middle of the night, unable to move, and think someone was in the room with me. Only the CPAP machine assured me I wouldn't suffocate, because even breathing seemed to stop during these episodes. I never knew when it was coming, and I never knew how to get out of it.

I also came to realize how many TV shows, video games, and movies revolve around violence. Every gunshot and gory scene caused me a physiological reaction. I'd either sweat, hyperventilate, or fight the urge to leave the room in a hysterical crying fit. Most times, when I felt a violent scene coming, I'd just close my eyes and think about that stupid painting on the wall at the hospital.

Flashbacks are real. They aren't just something the most shell-shocked combat veterans experience. Some images never leave you, and that doesn't mean they're hiding in your mind to retrieve when you want to reminisce. They're demons occupying space in your mind, and they'll remind you of their presence whenever they damn well please. For the first two or three weeks after the incident, that snapshot of what was left of Chip's head would pop into my head unprovoked, multiple times per day. These episodes did lessen over time and therapy sessions, though. Improvement came at the pace of a glacier, but just as steadily. Like the markings of a child's height on the kitchen wall, I'd only be able to see the growth in retrospect.

CANDACE'S MEDIEVAL FESTIVAL TOOK PLACE LESS THAN TWO weeks after I watched Chip Smith paint the ceiling red. I used the incident as a reasonable excuse not to attend, and she didn't push back at all. We'd all gotten a week off from school for mental health reasons, which the school district recognized as necessary (go Missouri!). There was no such mercy for the second week, though. And it sucked. In health class, we talked about the warning signs of suicide and all the right things to do if we see them. Everyone spied me from the corners of their eyes the whole time, as if I were suddenly an expert in the field. I wanted to throw my hands up and say, "*What?* You think it's *my* fault?"

But I didn't.

As the weekend approached, I had no obligations. Mom and Dad were sympathetic to my every mood, and schoolwork was bare bones. Candace didn't expect me to show up at the Renaissance festival, and I was fully entitled to a few days alone with my thoughts . . . and my PC. I had a golden ticket to indulge myself in the sanctity of primal nerdism on the interwebs. I'd looked forward to it all week.

On that Friday afternoon, when I stepped off the school bus, I should've felt a wave of overwhelming liberty. But as I trudged toward my family's trailer, something else overcame me. It wasn't quite a sense of *obligation*. Rather, it was this nagging sense of an opportunity I might miss. A *rare* opportunity.

I was entitled to copious portions of greasy pizza and a case of Pepsi all to myself, but still I felt inclined to throw the comforting blanket off my shoulders and *do* something. (Seriously—why are trauma survivors always comforted with a blanket and a cup of something warm? Do they still do this when something horrific happens in Arizona?)

I needed to show up at the Renaissance festival, and not for Candy's sake. The force drawing me there was not so much a push, but a pull. Why would I pass up such a chance to interact with the only girl who'd ever occupied my dreams?

There's only one answer: because I'm a dumbass and a coward.

But cowards don't survive what I'd been through. And dumbasses don't learn from their pasts. But I'd survived, and I was learning how strong I was. The odds were stacked against me, and sitting alone in my room for forty-eight hours doing whatever would only exacerbate those odds. I had a choice, and much like a bold move in one of my favorite RPGs (role-playing games), I'd seize the narrative.

After thirty minutes of watching cat videos on Instagram, I closed all apps and drafted a text to Candace.

> Hey your grace… or whoever you are lol. Life is trash but I think I might come to your midevil thing up in Kingdom City. Is that cool? Could I ride with you?

I hit send without proofreading. I knew if I took the time to analyze my words, I'd never send the message. Just as I was about to navigate away from the message center, I saw her contact picture fall down to my message—meaning she'd seen it. Then it showed that she was typing. Her message popped up within seconds.

> Lol I thought you'd never ask! I'm riding with my friend Barry, and your welcome to join us. He has a sweet van lol

She responded immediately, which bypassed social protocol this early on. A sweet van sounded amazing. It'd probably be no problem for my big ass to find a spot to sit comfortably. Suddenly, staying home and dwelling on my pain seemed like a loser move. After feeling like I had numerous options, I now felt like I had only one. I replied to Candace.

> I'm there!

Thanks to my earlier attempts to speak her dialect, I knew what her response meant:

> Gramercy!

But she was still typing. I gnawed on my lower lip in anticipation of whatever she was adding to her antiquated outburst of gratitude.

> I dont suppose you have any plate armor or chain mail that fits you? Lol
>
> Maybe just a noseguards helmet wou;d work [smiling emoji]

No, I did not have any of this. In fact, such things would probably cost hundreds—if not thousands—of dollars, which neither I nor my parents had to spend. I stared at her messages, my mind racing to come up with a response that wouldn't exclude me from the festivities, but also wouldn't put any sort of financial burden on her. Honesty had become my safe place, so I went there.

> Lol ummmm I'm quite large and also poor. I have none of these things haha

She seemed to be typing for hours. But when her message finally popped up, it was all too succinct.

> Don't worry. We'll get you battle ready lolz

I've never been battle ready in real life. At least, not in the literal sense. Figuratively, every single day had been a battle, so I was tried and true in that respect. If there were a joust of insults, I'd be impenetrable.

In the morning I had Dad drop me off to meet her at Barry's house, so they wouldn't have to see the shanty I called home. But as it turned out, Barry also lived in a trailer park—just a nicer one than mine. And if his van was *sweet*, Candace must have meant the interior (if she wasn't being facetious). The exterior looked like something that belonged in someone's yard, surrounded by overgrowth—the crimson paint was matte rather than gloss, the right-front fender was navy blue, and a spiderweb-pattern fracture sprawled across the passenger side of the windshield.

Only then did it become clear that Barry wasn't to be our *only* companion for the trip, just the wheels. Three other nerds and one other female (also a nerd) would also be in the van, which created problems. I actually had to cite my height and explain the fundamentals of center-of-gravity to the three dudes in order to win a seat in the middle row, rather than the far back.

Although Candace sat next to me for the three-hour drive, it was wholly miserable. The interior was surprisingly nice—it'd had a lot of work done—but the air conditioning didn't work. And it was really hard to look at her while talking, given the height difference at such close proximity. I was sure she'd lose all interest in me after this experience.

Then there was the festival itself. Unfortunately, I had to dress as a peasant due to the lack of any other costume availability. I know I was supposed to look pathetic, but somehow it felt like overkill to have me wearing grossly undersized clothes. I thought I was supposed to be an ogre or something—what'd happened to that? I'd much prefer to play a subhuman monster than a giant peasant in rags that left my knees and paunch exposed. I could feel the fingers pointing at me from a mile away.

Beyond this humiliation, I had no idea what I was supposed to do besides wander around. And since Candace was the Queen, I had no business being anywhere near her most of the time. One of the couple of times I tried to approach her, the royal guards (or paladins, or what the fuck ever) stepped in my way with their play weapons. I could've easily trampled them, but I didn't know what kind of faux pas that represented. So I opted for a less combative move, and tried to reason with them.

This was a mistake, given I couldn't speak the *Queen's English*, so to speak. They ended up escorting me to the stocks for public humiliation (as if I weren't becoming immune to the concept). Again, I could've easily broken free of their restraints, but I decided to play along. Bystanders jeered and thumbed their teeth at me (which I assume is insulting) all the way to the stocks. Once there, they tried to lock me in the arm and neck holes, but the stocks were so flimsy that I tried my best not to be the asshole who destroyed their silly props.

Once I was "locked" into the humiliation restraints, commoners began hurling "rotten fruits" at me—which were actually multicolored, water-logged foam balls. I supposed I felt humiliated, but the more important sensation was relief from the heat as the splashing water drenched my head. When people missed, I got angrier at them than the ones who hit me square on. I lapped what I could with my tongue, impervious to the salty flavor from mixing with my sweat. (Obviously, I'd tasted much worse in my recent past.)

Secretly, I'd also been expecting to be welcomed as a sort of celebrity there, given that my entire social media following had started with this crowd. A few chatty characters did come up to me and mentioned the video and my online presence, but were promptly admonished for breaking character by the more hardcore cosplayers. Others commented on my size in Old English in passing, but I couldn't be sure whether they were praising me, insulting me, or just making general observations.

In all, it sucked. I was hot and uncomfortable (in every possible sense of the word), and bored out of my skull. And the food was dry and flavorless (although free of charge) in the spirit of periodic authenticity. I couldn't help but scoff at all this uncompromising realism, which conveniently ignored the ubiquitous plastic water bottles everywhere. I guess they had to draw the line somewhere.

There were bright spots, though. While my only interactions with Candace were as a spectator of her greatness, Barry ended up being my lifeline to conversation—turned out, he was pretty cool. Dare I say it, we became friends.

He knew I was hating every second, and reassured me that Candace only invited me so I'd be impressed by how she was regarded there. That did make it all much more tolerable, I admit.

On the way home, Candace was pretty manic. Being worshiped twelve hours straight must really get the endorphins going. But then she picked up on my misery, and repeatedly swore she'd make it up to me somehow. And she kept touching my leg and my hand when she said so. But best of all, when she finally crashed, she fell asleep in my lap.

By the time Barry dropped me off at home, I'd decided that somehow—despite my exhaustion, dehydration, and frustration—it'd been worth it. I couldn't have known how right I was.

26

Things were improving, but all was not roses. I was on a critical mission to pursue my identity as a trauma victim, a survivor, and a work in progress. Erin had helped me look past my guilt, shame, and humiliation to actually talk about these things called *feelings*—a topic Ma and Pop included on the household taboo list. But for each step forward, there seemed to be five steps backward.

Details of Chip Smith's family and background came out in the following weeks, and it was impossible to discern hearsay from fact. The veracity of the claims almost didn't matter to me. Either way, each tidbit made me hate him less, which hurt me to the core. I *needed* to detest him. He *had* to be irredeemable. It was my only consolation.

The story about his mother turned out to be true. In a bout of bravery, I looked up the police report to confirm or debunk what I'd heard. She was killed in a drunk driving accident, and the Smiths got nothing in the form of civil restitution or life insurance, as was rumored. And, as Chip mentioned in his final moments, the reason for this was that Roscoe Smith was, in fact, the drunk driver in question. He'd been intoxicated three times the legal limit, but somehow made it all the way home. Mrs. Smith—Mimi, she went by—was doing laundry in the garage when Roscoe came home, barreling down their driveway recklessly. He mistimed his stop, then stomped the accelerator instead of the brake, smashing her body against the washing machine and cinder block wall at around thirty-five miles per hour. His truck pinned her dying body just as Chip came out to witness her death.

Trinity hadn't turned to prostitution after dropping out of school, though—that part was false. But, it turns out she was a horrible, vindictive, conniving bitch way before she'd been enlisted to torment me. Rumor had it that she tried to start a cult at age thirteen, and her kid brother was her first follower. He got mocked at school for everything she did at his expense, which was a lot. Trinity had always been the popular mean girl at school, and Chip wanted nothing more than to hitch his wagon to hers. From the way it was explained in a blog post by one of his former close friends in Mississippi, he'd been her mistreated pet. Her approval was more important to him than their parents, and she'd exploited this weakness for devious purposes.

She had an apparent obsession with shaming guys through nudity, which I didn't need an outside source to substantiate. When Chip was in fifth grade, she'd snuck a frontal nude picture of him in the shower and sent the photo to the girl she knew he had a crush on. Although he'd been prepubescent in those pictures, he never shook the reputation for a small penis, which Trinity gladly perpetuated well beyond his puberty phase.

The hardest part of learning all this was considering the possibility that Chip Smith had had it worse than me. I had a small world full of unified bullies, but until he and his bitch sister came along, all they really did was laugh at my expense. I don't know if anyone ever made him eat his own shit or held a gun to his face, but some of the stories I heard and read made me wonder if I'd gotten the sweeter deal between the two of us.

Of course, Trinity had her own origin story. Chip and I couldn't be so fortunate as to have a definitive bad guy (girl) to blame. Mimi had purportedly pimped her daughter out to truckers at the bars in exchange for cash or drinks, starting at a very young age. While this seemed extravagantly salacious, it fit with her apparent aversion to big guys like me, along with men in general. She was a very pretty girl (though she'd grown quite ugly in my mind's eye), yet she'd never had a real boyfriend. She'd once gotten suspended from school for nearly biting a boy's penis off behind the theater stage. (One might wonder why the boy didn't get in trouble for indecent behavior as well, but then stop wondering upon realizing this took place in Mississippi.)

Erin once stumped me with a simple question. "Why does there *have to* be a villain?" she'd asked. Obviously, my reflex was something along the lines of, "There doesn't *have to* be. There just *is*." But my answer was irrelevant, and she damn well knew it. The question stuck with me. As she damn well knew it would.

There *has* to be a bad guy because otherwise, I have to look inward and consider the possibility that *I'm* the root of my problems—or at least a party to them. Without someone to put on the other side of an invisible line and point at as the hated enemy, all eyes might turn to me. Erin asked that question because she's educated, experienced, and licensed to do so, but I give myself credit for picking up on it.

I could blame God that I'm genetically predisposed to be enormous. I could blame the entire student body of Chandler's Marsh High School for making my formative years the most miserable phase of my life. I could easily point to the Smith family as unequivocal villains in my story. And you know what? I wouldn't be wrong. Those people are all assholes.

But that's not my business.

I'm Chance Branch, commander of this body and mind, and I have ultimate control of my actions. This may seem elementary, but it's a hard truth that took me a lot of work to accept. I never had control over what was said about me. I never could've stopped the snickering as I walked by. But the whispering behind my back is only the concern of those doing it. When I woke up each day, I had a series of choices, and I chose to hide. I could've crushed my enemies. Hell, I could've been the bully myself. I could've done any number of things in response to my unfortunate start at being a human, yet for some reason, I chose to try and remain unseen.

In a six-foot, ten-inch, 440-pound body, topped by a beacon of curly red hair, I honestly believed I could hide.

What a dumbass.

27

CANDACE KLAUSS SOUGHT ME OUT AFTER THE RENAISSANCE festival, even though I'd reverted back to one-word replies and short-term ghosting—my phone had become a source of anxiety, so I usually kept it face down on the table, ringer off. I know she probably assumed I was a bit resentful about the unpleasant experience I had at the festival, and truth be told, some assumptions are accurate. I didn't resent *her* as much as the letdown it represented. I'd tried to go outside my comfort zone, and all that resulted was a lot of discomfort. But I couldn't explain this to her because I didn't even realize it at the time. All I could do was turn cold on her.

Nevertheless, she persisted.

One day during winter break, she showed up at my home unannounced. Her parents had bought her an old Chevy truck for Christmas, and she exploited her newfound mobility by making my trailer park her first stop. For some reason, Christmas made it very difficult for me to cope with Chip's suicide. All the songs, movies, and TV shows engulfing society preached joy and being a good person, none of which fit my headspace at that time. Chip's family would have their first Christmas without him. If I'd shown goodwill toward all mankind, I would've found a way to stop him from pulling that trigger. I tried not to come off sullen when I greeted Candace at the door, but there was no hiding it.

I let her stand outside on the steps for way too long. It might've come off as passive-aggressive, but I honestly didn't think to invite her in. We caught up on all the small, innocuous events in our lives, ever conscious of the elephant of prehistoric dimensions occupying our common world. But then—before I even invited her in—she broke through that barrier.

"It wasn't your fault, you know."

My breathing shuddered as I tried to inhale. There was no chance of hiding the tears welling in my eyes. "Would you like to come in?" I said. I wiped my eyes when she walked past me.

After brief introductions to Ma and Pop (which were much more favorable than the ones I'd shared with the internet), Candy and I made our way to my bedroom. By a stroke of amazing fortune, I'd cleaned my room that afternoon, after a week (or more) of Mom nagging me to do so. I even had a plug-in air freshener going. Furthermore, I'd just started reading George R.R. Martin's *A Song of Ice and Fire*—an extremely violent and disturbing narrative my tone-deaf parents had given me for Christmas—and the first volume lay open on my bedspread.

"Nice room," she said, panning around. Her eyes fixated on the novel spread open to the early chapters on my bed. She met my eyes with a stunned expression. "Is that the first *Game of Thrones* book?"

I'm not a big believer in guardian angels and all that holy stuff, but seriously—what are the odds?

"It is," I said, scratching my temple. "I like to read."

While this wasn't a lie, it . . . kinda was. Reading had always been an escape for me. Any springboard off of this cruel planet could tickle my fancy. But ever since the incident, I became overly sensitive to depictions of violence, which I found to be omnipresent in literature. Not so much in a way that it caused me to weep or have an *episode*, but in a way that I'd zone out and stare at the pages, following the words on them without actually absorbing the content. My mind would just wander back to that horrible imprint on my memory, and become feral. I'd "read" an entire chapter before I realized my thoughts had gone astray the whole time, and I'd have to try and read it again—often with the same outcome. Candy didn't need to know that I'd been stuck on chapter five all evening, and that I'd only made it a few pages in. And I hadn't even seen the show on HBO, so any elaboration beyond that paperback on my bed would give me away.

"You're so tidy," she said, looking around some more.

"And this shocks you?"

She chuckled and started to speak, but then a spirited argument broke out between my parents. She cut herself off with a wry smile. "Would you wanna go for a ride with me in my new truck? Well—new to *me*, anyways."

Of course, I agreed. She was the only girl I'd ever imagined myself being with, realistically, and now she was in my bedroom. I may have been in a depressive phase, but I wasn't *entirely* detached. We interrupted my parents' dispute to say goodbye on our way out.

Her truck was a two-tone, blue and silver early millennium Silverado 1500 crew cab. Freshly washed and waxed. I was never a gearhead or anything, but I could appreciate the beauty of her new (to her) machine. By osmosis alone, I'd absorbed a fair amount of casual automotive expertise over the years, and now was the only time such knowledge would prove useful.

"Crew cab—nice," I said as we shuffled across the gravel lot. "Looks clean. Those are aluminum alloy wheels. Is it a V-8?"

"Sure," she said, nodding. "It's a double-barrel 454 carbine with double-axle dual overhead cams."

I laughed harder than her, recognizing that none of that made sense. It was a word salad of redneck jargon. Her attempt to sell it was quite respectable. "Ah, yes. I can tell by the tailpipes," I said.

We laughed together in a way that could only happen with someone who understood me. Who I understood back. How trite all these hicks around us were. How cruel the world was to us. How hard we both tried to fit in when we were never supposed to. Beyond our satirical assessment of her truck, we said nothing of substance—but it was clear we got one another. As deep as the marrow in our bones.

As I got in on the passenger side, I knew she was my person.

Candy was *not* a good driver. I spent most of the adventure making sure my seat belt was taut enough to keep me from eating the vinyl dashboard when we inevitably crashed. She swerved from her lane, misread whether a traffic signal was red or green, and went entirely too slow on the highways and way too fast on the residential roads. I decided on that drive that if she and I ever ended up in a household together, I'd have to be the one to do the driving. And I hadn't ever driven at that point.

I tried my best to listen actively as she drove, divulging her own internal struggles. The synopsis I managed to extrapolate amid my fear of an untimely death was that being overweight was a tad bit harder for a female. Maybe she was right about that, and maybe not. I'd be no one to judge because I was far too concerned with the weight limits on the seat belts. I would've googled it, but my right hand was fused with the oh-shit bar overhead, and my left hand was hard at work bracing for impact.

Our meandering voyage put us on a course passing the high

school. She slowed down at its driveway, then came to a stop on the shoulder. We both remained silent, staring through the passenger window at the state-funded sanctuary for our mutual torment.

"It wasn't your fault," she said again. "I mean it. You do know that, right?"

I maintained my stare at that building as moisture clouded my vision. I sighed as long and hard as possible in an attempt to hide it. "I suppose," I said.

"Look at me," she said. I shook my head, but she insisted. "Chance. Look at me."

I rubbed my eyes before facing her, only to find tears in her eyes as well. "It doesn't matter," I said. I tried my best not to come off ornery or rude, but the subject was my most sensitive. "I don't care whose *fault* it was. I could've done something differently, and I didn't."

She used a knuckle to wipe a single tear away from the corner of her eye. "There's a lot of people who could say that, you know." Then she put her hand on my knee, and met my gaze. "A whole lot of people."

"I know," I said. And then, without warning from those little guys in my head, I broke out in unabashed sobbing. Then, as she leaned toward me, I stretched across the pickup's bench seat to nestle my face into Candy's collarbone and really cry it out. And I do mean *ugly* cry. As if the emotions of the past thirteen months condensed into one single catharsis, I wept to the point of drooling. I didn't know—nor care—how this outburst would be received. It had to happen, and this was most apparent. As I dragged my nose across her hoodie, leaving a snot trail on it, she wrapped her hand around the back of my neck.

"It isn't your fault," she said again. And she kissed the top of my head.

Going by significance alone, this was my first real kiss.

Trinity may have been the first female to plant her lips on mine and exchange some remnants of saliva with me, but that cannot count as my first kiss. No—a first kiss is a vulnerable display of affection, compassion, and reverence. It's a gesture of humanity, despite humanity not being quite so kind.

I don't care that Candy and I didn't truly lock lips until weeks later. She saw me at my lowest, weakest, and least appealing. Despite this, she kissed the top of my head out of pure kindheartedness. The footprint of a phenomenon existing only in my wildest dreams—the stuff of fantasies, which people like me were born never to know.

Love.

Now, by the sordid series of events resulting from my choices—as well as the choices of others—I struggled to cope with the death of my obvious boogeyman. Chip was an asshole, through and through. But could I have reached him? What if we could've ended up friends? I'd imagine us sitting at a bar, reminiscing our tumultuous story among oblivious, drunken strangers. We'd been such sworn enemies, but our humanity brought us together in the end. I said just the right thing in the boys' bathroom that day, and because of it, we were both there to tell the tale. I'd order another round for the both of us. *Cheers*, we'd say. We might even fight tears as the booze tore our masculine defenses down. Part with a hug, even. Tell our kids the story of how our friendship began.

What if?

Those two words will haunt me forever, just as poignantly as the taste and texture of shit in my mouth, or the sight of Chip's brains on the ceiling. This might seem like a curse, but I wouldn't change a thing. The little doses of dopamine I always sought didn't equate happiness. It might seem fulfilling to lead a group of users in World of Warcraft or spend my days aggressively doing as little as possible. Fat, salt, and sugar often felt like the best life had to offer. But the truth is that it all has a low ceiling. Sometime during Christmas break of senior year, I surpassed that point. None of it mattered anymore. Visceral pleasure felt numb, and I wanted—no, *needed*—more than that. I just couldn't figure out what.

Therapy made it clear that I could never turn back the clock. I couldn't bring Chip Smith back to life and share a beer with him. I couldn't go back to second grade and use my size to terrorize the shit out of the snarky little assholes poking fun at me on the playground. As we allow the past to happen, we relinquish our control over it. But we always have domain over how it affects us.

And that is the hard part.

It wasn't a steady climb to sanity after Chip died. Erin didn't cast a magical spell to pull me out of my funk. In fact, for the first time in my taxing life, there was a point I considered ending myself. Maybe I'd be better off with my own brains blown out, I thought. These considerations were fleeting, but they kept me in check. Exhausting as this pervasive reflection might've been, I always knew where I stood among the world's participants, but more importantly, among the committee of guys inside my head. They never left that room each day without knowing why they'd shown up to work.

Sometimes it felt like the board would've been unanimous in euthanizing myself without that one last vote. I stayed alive because that one guy in my mind's headquarters refused to waver. *This is not where our story ends*, he'd say. *This is where it begins.*

I think the most frightening revelation of my psychological recovery was that my mental health was intrinsically linked to my physical health. Erin assured me this didn't mean I had to become a skinny vegan, which I staunchly dismissed as lip service. I lost a lot of trust in her when she recommended I go for a twenty-minute walk every day. *That's how they suck you in,* I thought. *Oh, it's not like you're going to the gym or anything! Just go for a* walk! But eventually, with three sessions a week, she wore me down, and I went for a stroll with her.

That walk exhausted me on every possible plane. Physically, twenty minutes (which was actually twenty-one) felt like a marathon at that skinny bitch's casual pace. Emotionally, this made me very sad. Psychologically, it all flashed me back to my football days. I joked about it, but Erin actually validated that it may have hidden as one of my first real traumas. I'd tried to become the one valuable thing the world thought I could be, and hated every second of failing at it. It was among the first moments I'd accepted that I had no value. I couldn't even make it back to Erin's office before I started sobbing, and she gave me what had to be the sweatiest, grossest hug of her professional career.

She created a tradition of kicking our sessions off with these walks when weather permitted, and a strange thing happened. I *liked* them. It felt good to get moving. To experience muscle fatigue. To sweat on purpose. It was way easier for me to talk about tough things with her with both of our gazes locked on the passing sidewalk below rather than sitting face-to-face in the phony hominess of her office. I began showing up to therapy in athletic gear, towel draped around my neck. She gave me an old Fitbit of hers, and I obsessed over my movement metrics. It became a game I could fixate on to escape and avoid the burden of everything I carried.

By the end of January, the needle started to move on my numbers. I lost eight pounds, lowered my blood pressure to the *middle* of stage two hypertension (a potentially lifesaving improvement), and I surpassed my goal of five thousand steps per day. I'd stare at the number, recalling how impossible it'd felt when I'd first gotten the Fitbit. But even on a qualitative level, walking got easier, as did breathing, sleeping, and putting on shoes. I passed up extra portions, snacks, and sweets on a more frequent basis, only partially for fear of undoing my progress—the real deterrent was just a lack of temptation.

The most notable change in my behavior was my participation in P.E. class. Good thing, too, because that semester was my last shot at completing the credit to graduate on time. I discovered that I was actually pretty decent at basketball, once I honed my dribbling skills a bit. It wasn't just my height, either—I could shoot, and I learned to use a couple charging fouls at the start of each game to get in my opponents' heads. My size did work to my advantage, though. I was a monster on defense and rebounding due to my height, and none of the normal-sized pipsqueaks could block my shots. Then, volleyball started, and I connected the dots that my size could be advantageous in almost *anything* I set out to do. All I had to do was figure out how.

The hikes took up more and more of my appointments with Erin, until one day when the walk consumed the entire fifty-five minute session. The next time, she made me sit for the session and told me to get a personal trainer. I laughed, because this was in line with her gentle sarcasm, but she assured me it was no joke.

Since it'd been deemed a medical necessity, I was able to find a trainer covered by insurance—a grown man named Skippy. Whether it was a nickname or his parents were actually mean enough to put that on his birth certificate, I never found out. In fact, I was never 100 percent confident Skippy's certification was authentic, or even that he knew what the hell he was talking about. He misused terminology and mispronounced words he damn well should've heard out loud as a supposed expert. (For example, he kept referring to walking as *calisthenics* and pronounced the word *endocrine* "*en-DOCK-rin*.")

His clinical expertise notwithstanding, Skippy taught me what might be the most important thing I've ever learned: how to appreciate discomfort. Not only did I grow accustomed to the pain of exercise, I became *slightly* addicted to it. The strength metrics of my actual body slowly replaced the virtual attribute levels of my video game avatars.

This alone might've changed my dad's thinking on therapeutic psychology, since he witnessed my physical and mental transformation firsthand. But what sealed the deal was the day I came home from a session and asked if I could bring a dog home, since Erin thought it a good step in my ongoing recovery. Of course, despite Mom's backing, his first answer was no, because Dad never said yes to anything right away, as a long-standing policy. When he relented, he asserted himself as a full—if not primary—participant in the selection process.

At the rescue, he zeroed in on an adolescent puppy with floppy ears and a long snout—some mixture of hound and lab—as though he were reunited with an old friend. The pup seemed just as familiar with Dad, wagging her tail the instant they met eyes. While we waited for the attendant to open the cage, I read the dog's name and lost my breath.

Candy.

I know, right? No effing way.

I've never been good at math, but I did my best to try and figure out the odds that my new dog would have the same name as the girl I was diffidently falling for. My conclusion was subjective but conclusive. The probability was astronomical. I laughed out loud pondering the possibility it was just a happy coincidence.

Yeah, right, I thought. *Fat chance.*

CANDY THE DOG WAS NEVER TRULY MINE, AS LONG AS DAD was around. But she certainly did her job helping me stay sane as I forged my new self. She also made Dad happy and enlightened him to the brighter side of psychotherapy, so I'd say she went above and beyond the terms of her employment. Sure, she pissed the rug sometimes and loved to chew shoes, but she earned her keep.

I felt comfortable reaching out to Candy the Girl to share my adoption of Candy the Dog, complete with a selfie of the two of us—my first selfie ever. As it turned out, Candy the Girl adores dogs, and proposed that we meet for a "dog date" at the dog park. Candy the Dog and Candy's dog—a mutt named Gandalf—got along swimmingly, allowing me the time I needed to brave the uncharted territory of charming a girl.

Undoubtedly, I was an awkward mess on that "date." But I must've done something right, because Candy and I ended up going to senior prom together, where we shared our first *real* kisses—by anyone's definition. I decided Trinity didn't count as a kiss, and while Candy kissing me on the head was important, it didn't meet all the criteria necessary for the record books. Candy admitted her first kiss story had been a total fabrication—her friends, followers, and even her parents all believed that she'd locked lips with a handsome baron at one of her festivals three years prior. I was the only one who knew the secret.

It's hard to decide whether the high point of my high school experience was linking arms with Candy as we made our entrance at the dance, or seeing those measurements when I got fitted for my tuxedo. Sure, the cheering was louder in the school gymnasium, but only to those who couldn't hear the guys in my head when I heard my waist size when I got tailored for my tuxedo.

I admired my dapper self in all three mirrors while the salesman waited patiently. I couldn't hear Mom raving about how handsome I was over the sound of me thinking it myself.

How could this be the same person from a year ago?

And really, how much was different, from where I stood? Sure, I'd shed a bit of girth off the edges, but I was still far from an Adonis. I looked good in that tux, but who doesn't? And yeah, it did great things for my looks and peace of mind that I'd started letting a licensed barber give me a legit fade. But my ability to stare in the mirror that long had little to do with my appearance.

Fun side note: renting a tux was not an option for me. My dimensions required a custom fit, which essentially doubled the cost. I watched the salesman tally the numbers for the final amount and knew for sure there was no way. We'd have to see what the big-and-tall store could throw together.

"Let's do it," Mom said, extracting from her pocketbook the thickest stack of cash I'd ever seen. She put the money on the counter and flashed a proud grin at me.

"Ma! Where'd you get that? That's way too much for a suit."

"It's worth it," she said, her eyes welling.

"Ma'am, this is just a quote," the salesman said, sliding the pile of money back across the counter. "You don't have to pay until the tuxedo is tailored and ready."

Mom started to reach for the cash, but I tapped her hand and addressed the salesman. "Maybe it's better if she pays up front," I said. We shared an awkward laugh, and the salesman walked away. "Where the hell did you get that kind of money, Ma?" I whispered.

"I hit the cover-all on Friday," she said, tickling her upper lip with her tongue. I knew this meant she'd hit the biggest jackpot at bingo. Depending on which church she'd scored big at, the prize could be as much as three grand.

"Ma . . . we have so much to pay for."

She raised her eyebrows. "More important than this? Listen, son—we'll take care of the bills, don't you worry about that. But you're becoming a *man*, you understand? And I want you to be better at it than your daddy. Besides, you can use this tux the rest of your life. You could wear it to your wedding!"

The way her eyes glimmered saying that last piece made it a done deal. As much as I looked forward to Candy seeing me so spruced up, Mom looking at me with such pride would change the way I viewed her. In fact, it already had.

My confidence peaked that summer, bringing on a decision that surprised no one more than myself. Bolstered by the intoxicating courage of a semi-romantic relationship, muscles that bulged when I flexed them, and lingering questions about what to do with my life, I decided to train for a shot at playing football for Mizzou. My quest to become a walk-on left tackle for the Tigers fit nicely with the Fat Chance trend (because the odds were certainly slim), expanding my presence on video-centric platforms like TikTok and YouTube. My workout videos gained a following of their own, which forced me to honor my daily grind. The results were visible, both in my performance and appearance—the latter of which was evidenced by the before and after photos I posted to all platforms the day before I traveled to meet the head coach on the University of Missouri campus up in Columbia.

Coach was impressed by my size, as expected. But he warned me that playing at the collegiate level was a big jump from high school ball, and size was only one of many requirements for an offensive lineman. In our email exchange, he'd asked me to bring film of my varsity highlights to our meeting. I refrained from disclosing that I'd quit midway through sophomore year, hoping to wow him with my viral workout clips instead. Dad told me on the drive there that this wouldn't suffice.

And he was very right.

The coach squinted at my phone as I held it in front of him, cycling through the best footage I had from my library of trending videos. He made me repeat the confession that I hadn't played either of the last two years of high school, and told me to put the phone away. My internet influence failed to impress him, and I'm sure it didn't help that I'd sweated through my collared shirt by the end of the meeting. With the disclosure that I'd not yet gotten my acceptance letter to even *attend* the university, he rose and shook my hand, wishing me the best of luck.

My soul was crushed. I easily could've complained, but I didn't.

I *couldn't.*

Two years prior, I'd been well on my way to an abbreviated and unfulfilling life. I'd gotten blessed by so many curses in the meantime, and now reaped the rewards. Now, even with my short-lived dreams of football stardom shattered, I could do the unimaginable. I could smile at myself in the mirror. At last, I could fathom the next day being better than the one before. I could cry—as I did on the drive home.

In front of my dad.

Nevertheless, my disappointment at the rejection from Mizzou ran deep. The tears had gone dry, but Dad and I hadn't said much since they flowed. On the last major stretch of highway before home, he decided to break the ice by making me cry again.

"Chance, I'm proud of ya, boy." His breathing shuddered as he inhaled, showing me rare vulnerability. "I know I don't say it enough. And hell, if I'm being honest, it never seemed like you cared. Never really did anything to *try* and make me proud before, ya know?"

That last little jab helped me compose myself. "I know, Pops."

"Nah, I didn't mean it like that," he said, waving a hand at the dash. He knew the sour message I'd take from that. "What I'm saying is, I know your life ain't easy, being built the way you are and all that. But I always wanted you to do something hard on purpose. Because you *chose* to. And not just to impress me. I want that for you because it's the only way you're gonna make it in this fallen world we live in. Course, the Democrats *want* you to be weak and dependent on—"

"I get it, Pops," I interjected. If I didn't steer our mutual train of thought, this important conversation would be over. "I think I never tried anything difficult because I was afraid to fail. To disappoint you and Ma. And myself. It just always feels way safer to not try anything, ya know? That's one of my many defense mechanisms."

Dad groaned, but also shrugged. "Sounds like more of that

psycho-babble that head shrink is teaching you."

"Pops—"

"Now, hold on. I wan't done talking. I was gonna say, whatever that egghead lady is teaching you must be working. Everything that's made me so proud of ya, you started doing after talking to her. I appreciate that, even if she's a leftist."

I pinched the bridge of my nose. "Erin isn't a leftist, Pops."

"Well, irregardless, she's alright by me. For what she did for this family, I might even send her a Christmas card or something." He glanced over at me, and we both erupted in laughter. Whether he'd been serious in saying this or not, we both knew damn well he'd never sent anyone a Christmas card in his life, and never would. His smile grew so big I got a rare glimpse of the metallic fillings at the gum line of his canines. The unspoken hilarity perpetuated, and we both laughed until we coughed.

Only then did I realize how seldom Dad and I had a laugh together. Our senses of humor were so different, but it still shocked me I couldn't think of a single other time we'd shared a moment like this one. As our fits died down, I resolved to have more laughs with him. It felt so good, but also so healthy. A rare and coveted combination.

I ALWAYS HAD THIS THING WHERE I FELT GUILTY ANYTIME I WAS happy. Maybe it wasn't guilt, exactly, as much as a sense that something bad was bound to follow. I'd started drinking young and learned very early on that a hangover was the punishment for my jolly time the night before. If I was playing video games, I should feel bad because it was rotting my brain, as they say (*they* being my grossly uneducated parents). But most of all, eating made me very happy, but society's punishment for that happiness never ended. It got to the point where I associated happiness with *unhappiness*, like I was the byproduct of some kind of unethical psychological experiment.

So as Dad and I exchanged jokes on the drive home, I paid no mind to the sinking feeling in my gut.

We turned into the lot, and the smiles disappeared from both of our faces. "Who the hell's car is *that?*" Dad said. "And where the hell is your mom's car?"

I stared speechless at the red Pontiac Sunfire. My mind did some quick math to estimate the odds of it being a coincidence, but then I noticed the telltale dent in the left rear fender. *Trinity.* The only question that remained was why it was parked at my home. I knew my dad thought it belonged to a man my mom was cheating on him with, so I did my best to reassure him. "I know whose car it is," I said.

Maybe she was here to make peace. Closure. Something along those lines. Perhaps this was part of her own therapeutic self-discovery, to make amends and all that. But as the car's door opened and she emerged, my soul gave me much more ominous signals.

Dad got out first, so I followed suit. He yelled something at Trinity, but his words garbled as my senses focused on other more important details. Her shoulders hunched high, despite her slumped posture. She was stick thin, like she hadn't eaten in weeks. The dark circles under her eyes suggested she hadn't slept in just as long. Her hair was greasy and matted, and her clothes stretched loose, like she'd been wearing them to bed for several days.

Even as my heart pounded with fear of what she might do, I tried to wrap my brain around the hypnotic infatuation I once had with her. In my eyes then, she was flawless. Now, she looked neglected enough to require medical intervention. But before I could dig deep enough to feel sorry for her, my eyes locked in on the shiny black object in her right hand.

"I asked you a question, bitch," Dad barked. "Just what the hell are you doing on my property?"

She didn't so much as look in his direction. Her eyes gazed only at me, dead and empty. I tried to read her expression, and my first thought was that she might cry. This didn't jibe with the gun she held along her skinny leg, but it's what my gut told me. Her voice creaked, like it'd gone weak from being idle too long. "You killed him."

Although I knew what she said, her words weren't loud enough for Dad to hear. He shouted at her louder to prompt her to do the same. "The hell'd you say? Speak up! You're trespassing right now." I felt him turn in my direction, though I didn't dare take my eyes off Trinity. "Chance, call the cops. And then go in and get my shotgun." I glanced over at him on the phone, already in the process of calling 9-1-1 himself.

How Dad didn't see the gun in her hand, I'll never know. It'd always been a sordid fantasy of his to shoot a home intruder, as we were reminded every time he renewed his NRA membership. Yet here we were, face-to-face with a violent threat at our home, and all he had in our defense were words of hollow bravado. Trinity raised the pistol, and leveled it at me.

This had to be a dream. It would make sense of Dad laughing so hard with me. Maybe the whole interaction with the coach at Mizzou was part of it, too. I waited for reality to pluck me out of this nightmare, but it never did.

Dad yelled a stream of expletives and charged at Trinity. I blinked just as the shot rang out. Dad collapsed in a heap at her feet.

My own calm surprised me. It didn't make sense that I'd just be standing there, watching this happen. It could only be a figment of my imagination. If my dad had just been shot, I wouldn't just stand there, breathing and watching as if it were a movie scene. But that's exactly what I did.

I told myself to attack her. To test the theory that this wasn't real. If she kills me, it was all a reality I could never face anyway. Otherwise, I'd simply wake up. But I couldn't move. All I could do was stare at Trinity's face, slack with catatonia and wet with streams of tears as she turned the gun in my direction. Just as I was about to charge, I heard Dad groan a stream of curses and threats.

He was alive. I couldn't die if he didn't. As Trinity meandered toward me, pointing the gun at my face, I realized this was no dream. It wasn't a clue that told me so, but rather a sensation. This was reality, and a gruesome version of it. Everything went quiet.

She pulled the trigger. I heard the shot, but never felt it. The only indication I'd been hit was how quickly my big body fell flat on the gravel lot.

VERY FEW PEOPLE HAVE THE PRIVILEGE OF REFLECTING ON their own deaths. For most, it's too quick—car accidents and heart attacks lend little opportunity to grasp what's taking place. For others, it's shrouded enough in dementia, delirium, or narcosis that they never truly *experience* it. But even among those who do, I wonder how many have been fortunate enough to have the time-bending moment I did.

To say *my life flashed before my eyes* would be a cliché mischaracterization of what went through my mind—other than that 9mm bullet. Yes, there was a flash—the gun's muzzle flashed. Yes, time slowed down. But the rest of my life was an afterthought. All that mattered—as in, truly held substance—was who I was in this moment of reckoning.

I never felt so stripped bare in all my living days. Even when I'd been disrobed in my sleep and displayed for the ridicule of the student body and all digital humanity, I'd never been broken down to my very essence the way I was the instant I resigned myself to destiny.

So much gets erased. When we meet the end of our stories, we lose all the details and become whatever summary we made of our lives. The bulk of what once meant so much gets blown away like dandelion seeds, leaving only the stalk to proclaim our place in the world. This journey starts with a set of circumstances. I could easily make the argument that mine sucked ass. But now, all that remained of me was what I'd done since that handicapped start.

My physique felt light for the first time ever. Only then was I enlightened to a startling truth—one I wished I'd had the capacity to ingest all my life with the same voracity as the foodstuffs that eased its pain.

I am not my body.

The shackles that kept my soul confined had been an illusion all along. I could've been anyone. Why wasn't *I* the bully? If humans were feral, I'd be the peerless alpha with such a ridiculous size advantage. All those years, I could've chosen to be the bold personality I became only out of desperation and despair. I could've shown myself to the world with reckless abandon so many years ago, tempting them to hurt me when I knew I'd grown impervious. This ugly meat suit I wore all my life could've been my strength, but I chose to embrace it as a hindrance. What a gutless idiot I'd been.

At least I understood in the end, though. Better late than never, right?

The familiar scent of blood hit me first. I forced my eyelids open and strained my eyes to look over at Dad. Only a small trail of blood oozed from the oblong hole on the side of his forehead. His eyes stared sleepily at the ground, blank and unfocused. He was definitely gone. I felt my own pulse quicken, thumping through my temples. I heard the fading crunch of feet on the gravel; then, I stared at Dad's body as heavy silence took over. I tried to say goodbye, but I couldn't form the words.

Just before I lost consciousness, I noticed a break in the quiet. Flashes of orange flickered on our neighbor's windows.

I strained my eyes toward our trailer, only to find bright flames escaping through the windows. Candy the Dog yelped, and I could do nothing to help her. I heard Trinity's garbled voice, most likely taunting me, even after all she'd destroyed.

Dad was dead. My home was burning, with my dog still in it. I felt completely comfortable closing my eyes with the certainty I'd never open them again.

The afterlife was surreal. It was like a vivid dream—so viscerally plausible, despite a deluge of strange and contradictory information. Spider webs, occupied by large, hairy tarantulas adorned every corner of the off-white room, but the strangers with me didn't seem to mind them. The dozen or so anonymous companions milled about and sat at tables, some of them engaged in board games. Chess, maybe?

I expected it to smell better. The room smelled sterile, yet somehow pungent. It reminded me of the scent of tire air—that stench of stale air that'd been trapped in rubber under pressure for a long time. I hated that smell.

Then a disconcerting detail struck me. I couldn't see any of the strangers' faces. No matter where they were, they managed to be turned in such a way as to hide their identity. When I moved to get a glimpse of one, the whole room reoriented to keep everyone facing away from me. I demanded that someone face me, but they all ignored me.

One character close by stood still, which made him stand out. I crept up behind him with the intention of surprising him. He was as tall as me, but thin, like Abraham Lincoln. I grabbed his bony shoulder and spun him around. My face froze in shock.

It was me. But skinny.

His (*my?*) cheeks caved in around the bones, giving the appearance of disease or malnutrition. I looked into his sad, baggy eyes and waited for him to say something—but there was no need. I knew what he had to say. That I should feel lucky for the life I'd had.

I tried to speak, but all I could do was shake my head. Sporadic loud beeps distracted me. I looked around to find their source, but couldn't. Only then did I notice that no one else was in the room—including the giant spiders. Then, a terse female voice blared.

"This got dang thing's been wonky since I got here," she said. The voice then mumbled unintelligibly before speaking loudly again. "Oh, hang on a sec! I think our big boy is making his way back from Neverland."

I managed to peel my eyes open despite them being taped shut. Harsh fluorescent lighting welcomed me back to consciousness. My throat burned. I tried to call out for help, but my vocals didn't work. After blinking the heavy film away, I spied the flurry of activity all around me. Medical people in scrubs of blue or crimson tended to things on all sides of me.

But none of them seemed to be paying any attention to *me*, exactly, until one of them grabbed a plastic monstrosity protruding from my mouth. The nurse said something to me with her face just a few inches from mine, but I didn't catch it. All I heard was her saying, "Okay?" I knew the only correct answer was yes, so I nodded. Then, on the count of three, she pulled it out. It felt like she pulled my entrails out with it. I gasped for air, horrifying myself with the screeching sound. But at last, I took in a full, cool breath.

I coughed until I gagged several times. This was disconcerting enough, but I noted that my attempt to cover my mouth registered nothing. Sitting up would make my situation much better, so I tried that. But again, nothing happened. It wasn't that I was too weak, or that it hurt too much—I just had no way to deliver the command to my body.

The nurse was very nice, but I couldn't make sense of her words. All I could gather was that the doctor would be there any minute to fill me in on what'd happened to me. I wanted to ask her why she couldn't just tell me herself, but forming words was still beyond my capability. She told me to *hang tight*. Like I had any choice.

I didn't need a doctor to be the one to tell me I was paralyzed. I knew.

32

As I waited for the doctor, the details of what'd happened started hitting me in waves. I stared at the pocked ceiling panels held in place by an orderly grid while I tried to absorb the death of my dad. And my dog. The bizarre scene from what I'd thought had been the afterlife still hung in my mind, and part of me hoped my dad's murder was just as fictional. But as the haze of everything else blew away, the ominous stalk of reality remained.

I knew the doctor when I saw her coming. While she didn't fit what I'd expected, her demeanor left no doubt. Granted, I'd still anticipated an old white guy with glasses and that reflector thingy strapped onto his head, as though I were in a 1960s cartoon. But the true character I knew was that of a doctor is of a decisive, overworked, conscientious overachiever. Although she was young, Black, and female, she fit the description of the latter.

Some doctors have a terrible bedside manner, but that alone isn't a deal breaker. *House* was a TV show centered on a good doctor with the bedside manner of a hitman, but 100 percent of people would say they'd prefer a doctor that proficient if their lives depended on it.

Other doctors have a great bedside manner, but they deliver

bad news the same way they deliver nasty medicine. They tell you something will cause "some discomfort," only to let you discover the sadistic truth for yourself. All trust is gone when you see through the mask of one of those bastards.

Dr. Leslie Harrison was a beautiful mixture of these. She was competent enough to understand that a good bedside manner could mean the difference between life and death for someone in my position. Delivery of the news that I was paralyzed from the neck down—and might very well be for the rest of my life—required just as much careful precision as anything a brain surgeon does. It calls for a level of salesmanship that could earn her a similar income at a Porsche dealership.

It's more than words. The air of positivity means everything, and I ate up every little promise that we'd be "in this together," even though I didn't know what that meant, materially speaking. But beyond that, her confidence made me feel safe. There was a range of percentage chance that I might regain use of my upper body, and I just knew she'd make it happen if it was in the cards.

She informed me that I'd been in the Intensive Care Unit at the University of Kansas Health System—known colloquially as KU Med—for nearly a week. Dr. Harrison took admirable pleasure in telling me, amid my confusion, that I was "not in Missouri anymore," but Kansas. The bullet had fortunately— for lack of a better word—passed through a chunk of my brain stem, but missed my actual brain. That was the good news. The bad news was that it'd grazed my spinal cord just enough to hinder many of the signals my brain sent to my body.

Dr. Harrison's explanation was longer and more detailed, and it made more sense as she spoke it, but she emphasized how lucky I was that the gunshot wound existed as it did. Millimeters in any direction, and my life would be drastically different, if I survived at all. Paralysis was an unfortunate outcome. But the way she explained it, I couldn't have expected anything better unless I'd been shot below the neck.

When the doctor left, I asked the nurse if I was allowed to have visitors. I was, but only until 9 p.m. The clock in the room showed it was somewhere around eleven. The nurse, Edna, read my disappointment and assured me that my mother had been in and out a few times last week to check in on me, but never later than six or so in the evenings.

"Bingo," I said out loud.

Nurse Edna paused her duties to give me a strange look.

It turned out Mom was off the wagon and fully immersed in her gambling addiction, once again. Part of me wanted to judge her for losing her resolve. But then I reminded myself that she'd lost her husband, her home, and almost her son. She had to cope somehow.

It did sting that Mom wasn't there when I woke up, though. I felt more alone than ever before—which is pretty damn alone. And I get that she has work, and bingo starts right after and doesn't end until visiting hours are over. But . . . c'mon, Ma. *Priorities.*

Nurse Edna was kind enough to get my mom on the phone and hold it up to my ear, just to reassure me that the old lady did care. I'd say the conversation was just what I needed, but I couldn't understand most of what she said through her neurotic sobs and wails. Admittedly, her anguish did make me feel loved. But when the nurse hung up and left the room, I appreciated the solitude.

Over the next day and a half, my condition improved enough that I was moved to a step-down room—where they move patients after the ICU. At KU Med—this was a cushy habitat. The corner room had a full-size couch for visitors, if I ever had any, and windows on two sides that provided a great view of the Kansas City skyline. In my many lonely hours, I'd stare at the distant site of Arrowhead Stadium, wondering what might've been if I'd pursued a football career in earnest.

Tragic as my ordeal had been, the community was well aware of it and had rallied in my support. And said support was independent of my internet notoriety—the horror of what Trinity had done was enough to scare up a regional following. But Fat Chance fans out there were also well-informed of my plight before the shooting. One night, a nurse informed me, as she casually administered my meds and checked my fluid levels, that a crowdfunding campaign on my behalf had raised almost a million dollars.

"A *million* dollars? Are you sure?" I said.

She paused her duties to check her cell phone. Her head bobbed as she chuckled and showed me the screen. "You're up to $1.1 million now, Richie Rich." She put her phone away and changed my IV bag as though this news was peripheral.

I wished so badly to cover my face with my hands. "*What? Who* started the fundraiser?"

She sighed as though I was being petty, then pulled her phone out again. After scrolling a moment, she said, "Uhh . . . Candace Klauss. You know her?"

I answered by closing my eyes and laughing. Luckily, the nurse walked out before the joyful tears leaked out. I shouldn't have been surprised that Candy would rush to my rescue under the circumstances, but I was. Not that I thought her loyalty was insincere or that she'd shy away from me when I became disabled. It was more that I assumed everyone else gave up on my survival when I did, as I lay there waiting for my world to die. I guess I just forgot that the person I was had ever existed. I'd been reborn, and she was from my previous life.

Word got around, and the nurses all called me *Big Money*. This was fun for about a day, but I was disappointed when the nickname stuck. Needless to say, I'd had worse.

The second night after I woke up, Mom tried to come see me, but it was after visiting hours. Nurse Edna told me she tried to sneak her in, but the ICU front desk lady was a hard-ass and wouldn't let her in. Only then did I realize KU Med was a four-hour drive from Chandler's Marsh. Mom took eight hours out of her day to not get to see me.

I felt bad for ever judging her.

My glory faded, as part of me always knew it would. New sad cases came down from the ICU, and I became old news. Paralyzed and rich had been intriguing, sure—but it couldn't compete with a firefighter built like a god who fell seven stories and survived. The nurses checked on him a lot more than me, and I refuse to believe it was simply because his dozens of fractures and infected lacerations required more care. It was because he was hot.

The worst of these for me was the guy who'd been shot in the head and survived. I didn't like how he made me feel fortunate that my bullet had missed my brain. The nurses could joke around with me. I could pay attention to everything going on around me. This guy would never have such luxuries. From everything I overheard, I inferred that the young father of two would need around the clock care for the rest of his life, and would likely never have another lucid conversation with his wife or kids. I resented having to be grateful for my condition.

Soon enough, I was moved from the step-down room to a regular admission room, which I shared with another patient.

I'd always dreaded the idea of ever having a roommate, and this was the worst possible circumstance to have one. Brian had ALS and could barely talk. While this made things simple for me socially, it presented its own set of problems. He was present for my sponge baths, and when my bedpan was changed, and he experienced all the associated sounds and smells. The nurses' physical struggles to care for a body the size of mine only furthered my humiliation. That's a level of intimacy that transcends verbal intercourse, and I'd never know what his thoughts were because he never spoke to me. All I knew about Brian beyond his condition was that he'd gotten as many visitors as I had.

None.

Brian ended up getting moved to hospice care after just a few days, and I at last had a room to myself again. Sure, I felt bad about Brian going away to die, but the sooner it happened, the better it probably was for him. And I needed my space. All those years in that little squalid trailer, and I hadn't even appreciated the solitude I enjoyed every single day, with a room to call my own. I wasn't so sure I would ever have such a luxury again, so I savored it. Any minute, someone could come into that room to breach my privacy and solitude, possibly forever.

And that's exactly what happened.

33

I SAW CANDY THE DOG COME IN FIRST, WEARING A PECULIAR harness. Dragged behind her was Candy the Girl. She wore makeup, an ornate hairstyle, and—when she met my eyes—a broad smile. I wished I could sit up, but all I could manage was an agape mouth.

"M'lord," she said with a deep curtsey, pulling the seams of her pretend skirt out wide.

I was in no position (or state of mind) to go along with the medieval lingo. I had so many questions, and I had to spit them out. "Is that Candy Dog? How did she survive? Didn't the trailer burn down? How'd she get out? How did you get her in here?"

"Nice to see you, too, Chance." She chuckled, clearly cherishing my surprise.

Candy the Dog hopped at my bedside, her paws extended just enough for me to see them. I could hear her claws scratching frantically on the metal rails. After a conspiratorial glance at the room's entrance, Candy the Girl hoisted my dog onto the bed. Normally, I'd lean away from her wet kisses, but now I could only turn my head. I resigned myself to being completely covered in dog slobber, then started to cry because I couldn't wrap my arms around her, or pet her to let her know I loved her even more than she loved me. I thought about nibbling her floppy ears just to send her some sort of gesture. She collapsed at my side, baring her belly to invite the rubs I once gave her. Candy the Girl stepped in for me and did the needful.

"Dogs aren't allowed here," I said, unable to hide or wipe my tears. "How'd you get her in?"

"This is a service animal vest," Candy said, tugging on it as she continued the belly rubs. She took a big breath. "So, my parents got me an emotional support dog a few years ago when they found out I was cutting myself. I'm not sure how they found it, or how it got certified, but that dog was an asshole. All it cared about was food and it never paid attention to me. If anything, it made me more depressed. Anyway, we had an extra vest, and I figured this would work. And it did!"

As vulnerable as Candy and I had been with each other up to that point, the revelation of her depression and self-harm would never have come up before. Certainly not so casually. It was like some invisible wall between us had evaporated, and there were suddenly no more secrets.

Only then did I realize my ordeal may have impacted her, and fundamentally changed her. After all, she'd achieved her own high school coming-of-age victory, arm in arm with me, mere months ago.

From my earliest memory, people had hurt me. Even the ones who loved me. All along, I'd been conditioned to care how my presence in a room would affect *me*. How people in that room would treat *me* as a result of whatever was happening. *We're studying sea life? Here come the whale jokes. Fatty acids? How easily can this term be weaponized at my expense?* I went through my life like an abused child, always flinching out of fear of that inevitable next beating.

How much of my self-awareness had been displaced to

make room for this cancerous presence in my mind? How, after satisfying the state's dozen-year educational curriculum and passing its standardized tests, had I never learned the basic concept that *I matter?*

I'd become the polar opposite of a narcissist, whatever that's called. Anything bad that happened, it was probably my fault. Anything that turned out right was most likely a matter of pure chance, or should be attributed to others involved—but, in my mind, such instances had been erased from the record.

Moments before the shooting, Dad said it never seemed like I cared. That I'd never even *tried* to make him proud. That'd struck me in the moment, and that feeling came back to me now. Because he was right—I'd never set myself up for disappointment by trying to make him proud. I never considered the possibility that my dad wondered whether I *wanted* his approval or not. His perspective had never occurred to me, so even though his approval could've changed everything for me and so many others, this tragedy was the result. He was dead. Chip was dead. I was paralyzed. Trinity would probably spend her life in jail.

What if it had never been about me?

This question tugged hard on the back of my brain, as all what-ifs did, but I'd have plenty of time to process it later. At that moment, I had Candy the Dog and Candy the Girl in my presence, both showering me with approval and love. I asked my girlfriend to wipe the snot from my nose. As she did so without hesitation or comment, I knew she was my person— just as surely as Candy was my dog. (Especially now that Dad was gone.)

"Why all the makeup?" I asked. I had much more pressing questions, but I chose to take my own lesson and be an observer. "And the hair. You look beautiful, and I look . . . like a bum. A common *peasant*, I do declare!"

Candy belly laughed. "*I do declare?*" she repeated, doubling over. Her nostrils flared in silent laughter as she forced her next words out. "It's like you showed up at a Renaissance festival dressed up for a Civil War reenactment!"

I watched her bury her face in my numb legs and smiled like an idiot. When she finally caught her breath, I let the silence settle before speaking. "How did Candy Dog get out alive?"

She used a knuckle to carefully scrape tears from the outer corner of each eye. Her smile faded. "So . . . funny story," she said, swallowing hard and averting her eyes. "Not *funny* funny, but you know—*interesting*. As it turns out, that Trinity ho bag went in and got her out. I guess she cares more about an animal than you or your dad." She forced herself to look up at me.

I glanced down at my dog. "So . . . wait," I said. Candy could sense the gears turning in my mind. She focused on her fidgeting hands. "The trailer was on fire, and Trinity went in there and got her out? Why? How did she know to do that? Did she see Candy in the window, or what?"

She took another big breath. "Can't you just be happy to have your dog back?"

"Please just tell me what happened."

She fiddled with the blankets and avoided my eyes. "The trailer was burning, and Trinity went in there to save her. She heard her yelping and whatnot, and I guess she found the ounce of humanity in her that still existed. Anyway, she came out with Candy, then got arrested. The firefighters all made sure she was taken care of." At this, she nuzzled her face into Candy Dog's belly, tickling her with her nose.

I could barely speak. "Trinity saved my dog?"

It was weird, but I saw things as a fatalist in the moment. As if I'd been a member of the audience all along, I accepted that Trinity had to kill my dad, and paralyze me, just as surely as I knew Chip had to die. That was all in the script, and Trinity had played her role. But it didn't make sense to me that she'd risk her own life to save a dog—*my* dog—of her own volition. If anything—if she were in character—I'd expect her to let Candy burn to death, and savor my pain. I could imagine her recounting me the graphic details of my dog's slow death, or recording it for me to see with my own eyes. I could even picture her heartless sneer as she did.

This act of heroism had no place in my narrative.

"Apparently," Candy said. "And I guess she got a few nasty burns in the process. The way I see it, she should get used to it, considering where she's headed in the next life."

I looked down at Candy Dog's undamaged fur. "Why'd she do that?"

Candy shrugged. "Personally, I think she saw the chance to be a hero instead of a murderer, like she is. Shoot a couple people, you're bad. But save a dog from a fire at the end of it all, it evens out, ya know? I mean, she had the audacity to live stream herself after shooting two people and setting your home on fire. I swear, she's a certified sociopath."

"What was she saying in the live stream?" Even as I asked this, I knew I was nowhere near ready for the answer.

"Trust me, you don't wanna know. Mostly just crazy rambling, trying to make sense of what she'd done. It's been trending a while now, but I'm sure most people are like me and just skip to the part where she saves the dog."

I took a deep breath through my nose, enchanted by the stench of my alive and well dog's spittle infused in my stubbly mustache. "Can I see it?"

Candy scoffed. "I mean, you *can*," she said. "But why would you *want* to? She killed your father, Chance. Are you sure you're ready for that?"

"I want to see Candy Dog being saved."

She looked back at me, then raised her eyebrows. "Oh, you mean *now?*"

I nodded. Maybe I wasn't quite ready for what I was about to see, but I had to see it. It was actually a bit surprising the social media gods hadn't already deleted it, under the circumstances. So it was now or never, as I saw it. After some fumbling and fiddling, Candy found the appropriate place in the digital story, and held up the screen for me to see.

Trinity's tearful face consumed the small screen. Moments after shooting my father dead, and paralyzing me, she stared back at her audience with a modesty I'd never seen before now. Her eyes were unmade and puffy, the angle was unflattering, and the presentation was desperate from the start. Not desperate for likes or views—like the bulk of the internet—but thirsty for understanding. For empathy. Her tears were genuine, as evidenced by the snot bubble in the camera's foreground at one point. I could hear Candy Dog's cries before Trinity did, and my heart sank in terror, even though she rested safe in my lap while I watched.

It was hard to make out anything substantial amid the darkness of dusk, but Candy Dog's desperate howls were now loud and clear. Trinity whipped her head around to look back at the trailer, then whispered, "The hell? Who's that? There wan't no dog in there before!"

In response to the cry of an animal, Trinity had chosen to refer to it as *who* instead of *what*. In her emotional and psychological distress, she valued my dog's existence. After snuffing out a couple human lives (as far as she knew), she discovered her humanity.

The moral dissonance made my head hurt.

Trinity's face occupied most of the frame, so it was hard to tell where she was or what was going on. But I heard the telltale creak of our screen door just as she pulled her shirt over her mouth. At some point, the camera's perspective flipped to facing forward. After a confusing blur of motion in the smoky haze of my home, the scene got clear enough to see.

She charged into the first bedroom—my parents' room. And there lay Candy Dog, nuzzled in the corner where the smoke was the lightest. My breathing hitched as I watched my dog quaking in terror, one floppy ear laying along her snout as though trying her best to use it as a filtration device. I had to blink the tears away quickly to make sure I didn't miss a moment.

"Don't worry, pupper, I got you," Trinity said in the sweetest, softest tone I'd ever heard from her. It sent a shiver down my numb spine.

She scooped Candy up and turned to leave the room. After a terrified scream and a stream of cursing, the camera fell to the floor, showing the audience nothing but the fast-charring ceiling tiles of our single-wide trailer. The scene's thick, smoky grey faded to a featureless black, and Candy pulled her phone away.

"It's just five minutes of nothing after this, until her phone burns up." She took a moment to study my face, a worried expression on her own. "What're you thinking? Should I not have shown you that? Shit, Chance, I'm sorry."

"Nah," I said as reassuringly as I could. "It was good. It's all good." I had so many thoughts swirling through my mind, and I wanted to reassure the frontrunner for most important person in my life that she hadn't inadvertently hurt me. But I couldn't figure out what to say. It was all too much.

Candy wiped the tears from my cheeks. I asked her to put my hand on Candy Dog, and she did. I couldn't feel her plush fur, but I knew she could feel me. Part of me hoped she'd feel the dead weight of my arm and understand why I couldn't pet her—which wasn't far-fetched. She was a smart dog.

An all-business nurse came in shortly afterward and kicked Candy out for sneaking a dog in. She was nice about it, but policy was policy. After we parted with a kiss—as routinely as an old married couple starting their day—I lay alone in the room, staring blankly at whatever was on *Real Housewives of Wherever*. The dramatic turns of my real life distracted me from whatever shallow drama unfolded on the small plasma screen mounted high and far away.

A tear rolled down my cheek. I could feel it making its path under my chin and down my neck—and I could feel where my sensation ended. I wasn't even sure whether it was a tear of joy or sorrow, but it reminded me where I was at this point in space and time: alone, incapacitated, and numb. I asked myself a question so many times in my head that I ended up saying it out loud.

"Now what?"

34

CANDY BECAME A FREQUENT VISITOR THEREAFTER, USING the crowdfunding money to pay for a nearby hotel room. Mom visited a few times, and apparently had fun slumber parties with Candy, but she had to get back to her nine-to-five on weekdays. The steady flow of attention kept my spirits up after several surgeries to hopefully restore some mobility.

The prospect of being able to move again, even if just enough to pet my dog, motivated me. But the *post-surgery blues* are a very real thing. And Candy made it very clear to me that she'd stay by my side through thick and thin (for lack of a better idiom). Even if this early romance fizzled, she reassured me without words that it wouldn't change her loyalty to me. I knew we'd likely never consummate our relationship, but this experience left no doubt in my mind. I loved her, and I always would.

She also helped get me through the grueling tribulations of physical therapy. While psychotherapy had grown on me, and I still looked forward to my sessions with Erin, I never failed to dread physical therapy. It's just painful and difficult. Sadistically so. It's as if the whole field of study is based on the philosophy, "Find ways to cause pain without making the injury worse." (This makes the *do no harm* clause of the Hippocratic Oath a matter of semantics.)

Happy as I was that I regained hints of feeling and movement in my arms and torso, the physical therapists seemed to want to punish me for it. I became convinced the only people who would willingly do that for a living had to have been psychologically damaged in their formative years. It's a plausible theory, considering very few people escape adolescence without trauma.

Obviously, my limited mobility put a real damper on my video game aptitude, so I unofficially retired from the World of Warcraft in a goodbye message to my online friends that, looking back, was a bit dramatic. But I couldn't help myself—saying goodbye to that part of me was like a death all its own, and I thought a sappy speech was in order.

I'd grown tired of mindless TV from my extended hospital stay, and without video games, I became deprived of mental stimulation. Hobbits and Harry Potter somehow became less magical after my near-death experience. I think it had less to do with my handicap than it did with its link to my adolescence. I'd matured more since graduation than I had since middle school, so I was ready for the next level of exploration into literature. I actually *read* some of the classics we'd been assigned throughout high school, having only achieved a passing grade with the help of SparkNotes. (May God bless the brilliant soul who invented this resource. I owe them my diploma.)

As a result, I became a bona fide *reader*. It took very little motor skill to turn pages or scroll on my Kindle (thanks, Candy), so it got to the point where I consumed books in bulk. My curiosity went all the way back to Shakespeare (once again, thanks to Candy), and the simple fact that it was voluntary made it enjoyable. From that to Dickens and Brontë, all the way to Michael Crichton, Stephen King, and George R. R.

Martin (Candy insisted I read the books before watching *Game of Thrones* with her), I felt I'd earned an honorary English Lit degree. Eventually, given enough time, I would read everything ever written.

But then what?

The answer was to write. The best works of literature were planted firmly in my brain, so I should have all the tools to write my own masterpiece. But that way of thinking led to a rude awakening—my assumption was akin to an avid armchair NASCAR fan getting behind the wheel of one of those machines and becoming the next Dale Earnhardt. I might become great with enough practice, but I made sure to delete those first attempts at writing from the recycle bin, never to be seen again by another set of eyes.

I had a good vocabulary, though, so I made numerous attempts at fiction. The most daunting part is that every story idea possible has been done before. Every single one. So I took off my *online influencer* hat and instead subscribed to be influenced by experts in the field. The wealth of information and encouragement they provided me in my writing adventure made me feel more satisfied about my own online influence. How many obese people and social outcasts had learned to cope just because I'd decided to put myself out there?

Still, a decent story just wouldn't materialize in my imagination. Determined as I was to pen a fantasy novel, I sucked at it. And I don't say that out of humility or self-deprecation. It was all unreadable. Absolute trash. I wanted to give up entirely and make sure no one ever knew that I even tried.

Then, from thin air, a much better idea arrived in my mind. Like a magical quill floating down into my waiting hand from a golden goose flying overhead. I'd use it to pen a story more unbelievable than Hobbits, wizards, or magical dragon-riding monarchs.

My true life story.

Erin loved the idea because recounting my traumas with my current wisdom would help accelerate the emotional and psychological healing process. My physical and occupational therapists also applauded the venture because my fine motor skills improved markedly when I started writing. (I didn't disclose to them that I'd used a dictation app for the first draft.) Candy read my work right there in front of me, and I saw how it moved her—she cried numerous times, even when rereading the draft. She insisted I publish.

But no one loved the idea of writing more than I did. Though I'm paralyzed now, I feel more able than I had all my life because I finally had a voice. I'd much rather be wheelchair confined and heard than able-bodied and voiceless.

The final tally on my crowdfunding campaign came to $2.1 million. Of course, the funding platform and Uncle Sam took their share—but I was still a millionaire. I cut a check to Candy for half a million, since there was no way such a fundraiser would've come to be without her. Plus, if things went the way I hoped, it'd all end up in a joint bank account anyway.

Trinity's trial dragged on for over a year, but she sat in jail the whole time. The insanity plea proposed by the public defender had ultimately failed, but a loud part of me wasn't okay with this. The bitch was crazy. She'd only be a danger to society if she didn't get psychological help. Putting her in a human warehouse for the rest of her life seemed even more destructive. The District Attorney asked me to speak at the sentencing hearing, but I don't think it got the intended results. The problem was that he assumed I had a strong bond with my dad, and that I'd break down in tears speaking about his loss.

I didn't.

The truth was, Dad and my mom were good parents, but only inadvertently. They'd prepared me for a world that would treat me like shit, by treating me like shit—thereby desensitizing me to it. Sure, they loved me. But at no point in my existence did I think I was the most important part of their lives. Society wasn't going to dote on me, and I never had such an expectation. I can only imagine how hard life would've been if I'd been coddled. My folks loved me, but their inability to make that clear jaded me forever. Perhaps that was for the best. But—as Erin would say with a harmless shrug—perhaps not.

My Oscar chances were further dashed by the fact that I didn't hate Trinity. The way the young assistant attorney coached me, I should've been primed to deliver an emotional rebuke. But with millions in my bank account and a young woman who loved me, I had more at the moment than I'd ever had in my life.

Most importantly, little was missing.

The only time I got choked up was when I talked about my last conversation with Dad. We'd shared a hard laugh. He'd told me he was proud of me, and that he loved me. It would've been nice to live in a reality where he could keep saying those things, and Trinity had taken that from me.

But when I looked across the courtroom at her, all I saw was a defeated soul. Another badly damaged child. And her fate was in my hands. All I had to do was weep for my audience, and she might get the death penalty. I'd spent the vast majority of my existence trying not to cry.

So I did it one more time.

She was sentenced to life without the possibility of parole.

I guessed, based on the reactions of those around me, that this was a win. Some of the nameless faces in the gallery rabbled in protest that Trinity wouldn't be put to death, and I often think about those people. Who had hurt them?

All I saw in that moment was the empty look in Trinity's eyes. A life wasted. With a little compassion, she might've healed the damage done to her, including the harm done by herself. But now she'd be sent away to an even harsher place that would make her even angrier and more lost.

The lawyers walked out with handshakes and back pats, only because it'd have been in poor taste to exchange high-fives. I left the courthouse that day without comment or expression for the news people lurking outside. Part of me wanted to cry—and not tears of joy. But a bigger part of me just wanted the world to stop seeing this horrible saga and its characters as salacious entertainment, so I kept a stone face until I reached the safety of the van's tinted windows.

Closure is a sexy word people throw around. With Trinity's sentencing, I could close the book on this saga. How shortsighted is that? If you spent a moment in my enormous shoes, how could you ever see someone else's downfall as a pretty bow atop my story? I sat in the back of the wheelchair van, staring mindlessly out the window while I rehashed everything I'd experienced.

It all seemed so fanciful.

How could it be that an ugly, monstrous, morbidly obese ginger kid with a speech impediment from rural Missouri could rise to internet stardom, survive a gunshot wound to the head, and then become a millionaire out of the kindness of strangers? Sure, my dad was dead and I was mostly incapacitated—but ultimately, that would've been a safe bet for anyone who'd caught a glimpse of me as a toddler.

They'd never expect me to get the girl, though, would they?

Yet, many of them might've bet on me getting rich. After all, I had all the makings of a pro football player. But exactly zero bettors could've guessed I'd instead achieve financial independence getting shot by my bully's sister, and raking in my fortune due to the selfless efforts of a medieval cosplay nerd.

In all seriousness—what are the odds?

The world will forever recognize me as *Fat Chance*—not the slur people made of the shortsighted label fated to me at birth, but the name I made for myself.

What's in a name, indeed?

AUTHOR'S NOTE

IF YOU INSPECTED MY AUTHOR PHOTO CLOSELY OR INTERNET stalked me, you may have noticed I'm not morbidly obese (not as of the first edition, anyway). This story is in no way a memoir. Only a select few people know where I got the idea, and I may or may not keep it that way. (I hear an element of mystery about it will increase sales. And I do like money.)

That said, there are certainly autobiographical elements incorporated into many parts of this novel. I won't list them all, but I can divulge that as an adolescent I struggled with social anxiety, bullying, ridicule, normalized poverty, and an absurdly small high school population. My mom was a bingo addict, and my friends were mostly dickheads to me. But above all, I had a weight problem—the opposite of Chance's. As of high school graduation, I was a whopping 135 pounds—at 6'2" tall. People often thought I had rickets, a crack cocaine habit, or Marfan Syndrome (the thing Abe Lincoln had).

So, yeah . . . I'm an expert in the subject matter.

I'd be lying if I said this was a complete story when I dreamt it up. I'd just finished an epic rewrite of a previous (currently shelved) project. While it was with my editor, I decided to write a few short stories to publish. My goal was to create some free content to help build a readership. This story was originally two pages long in Microsoft Word—less than a thousand words. But much like the infant Chance Branch, it grew at an alarming rate.

I let it grow into an oxymoronic *long* short story until I looked up the threshold for it becoming a novella. Then, I tried to stay within *that* boundary; but Chance's experience took on a life of its own. I don't even know how I came up with half of this shit—thoughts arrived like butterflies, if that makes sense. I fell in love with my character and felt a bit like a method actor, truly living as someone else whenever I sat at the keyboard. A *method writer*, if I can coin the term.

After receiving my editor's feedback on my primary story—which was more than twice as long as this one—I was thoroughly defeated. Soon after, writing became a source of anxiety and insecurity. And this is not a dig at my editor at the time—that epic manuscript was *rough*. Trash, even. Then, I rewrote it based on the feedback, and this hobby/passion of mine began to feel like a job that didn't pay. No money, no satisfaction, nothing.

Quitting fiction writing felt like a very realistic possibility. Maybe just a break from it, leading to eventually quitting. Maybe just start a blog or something to feed the writing monkey on my back.

But as this story grew and I wrote it for the sheer joy and catharsis it provided me, I fell in love with writing again. When I finished the first draft, I shared it with my cousin, Darcy Lindner, who is *not* easily impressed by books. She read the whole thing in one day. That's when I knew I had something worth refining. Something that was truly mine that wasn't garbage. I wiggled in my seat and fixed my posture.

This became the first work of fiction I wasn't insecure about. It's almost spooky how much Chance's identity crisis mirrored my self-discovery as an author. I followed the Zero Fucks

Doctrine, and wrote without fear or hesitation.

I don't know if this book will sell or not. But in line with the ZFD, it doesn't matter. I don't care. This is a successful story because—whether or not it's as good as I think it is—I found my voice in the process. I'm almost as thankful for that as I am for your money. Either way, the hero of my own story wins.

ACKNOWLEDGMENTS

THIS IS MY DEBUT PUBLICATION, SO I'M NOT SURE OF THE right order to thank people. If I get it wrong, I'll learn from my mistakes in the future.

First, I have to thank anyone who parted with their money to read this book. Without that financial incentive, this story likely would've stalled early on, or been born prematurely, leaving so much unsaid. But most importantly, people who pay to read are the lifeblood of intelligence. With the decay of modern attention spans, the dedicated reader is a link to the millennia of human history where words matter.

Next, I have to thank my wife, the beloved Kate Norwalk. Without her support, my adventure to become an author could not have happened. But more specifically, *this story* could not have happened. She was there from its infancy, and cheered me on every step of the way. I'm so glad I decided to keep her around.

My kids come next because they're the only other OGs who knew about this story from the start, and encouraged me at every opportunity. As early teens and preteens, Luke and Savannah were most precocious to listen to my summaries of what I'd written on the drive to or from school, and spitball with me about them. To the reader—don't assume kids aren't ready to see your vulnerable side, or be involved with your grown-up adventures. You'll both be better for the mutual candor.

On that note, I must give an extra shout-out to my daughter, Savvy B, for rendering my original cover art. She has an eye and a vision that can't be taught. I've known her long enough to recognize that she was a born artist—for everything that means. I didn't outsource my cover design to a 13-year-old out of charity. I did it because she was up to the challenge. (And because the labor was dirt cheap.)

Darcy Lindner was my sole alpha reader—she read the first draft before I'd even taken a second look at it, and gave me feedback that completely changed the story. Without her input, this may very well have ended up a mediocre novella. Instead, it is whatever it is. She gets equal credit or blame.

My editor, Alex Thieme, was a perfect fit for me, and specifically, this story. There are editors who will lick your ass just to keep you happy, and others who will knock you down as many pegs as they can just to prove their own worth. I often felt like Goldilocks in my quest to find the right one. Alex has been that *just right* bowl of porridge, always maintaining my authorial voice, but objectively telling me when things didn't work, or needed revision. Is that not what editors are supposed to do? The best part is that I first hired her as a beta reader, and by the quality of her feedback, I knew she was up to the task of editing this text with the right touch. I never looked back. Sometimes, the stars align.

This is my first go at independent publishing, and I don't think it would've been quite as manageable under my time constraints without Ryan Forsythe's expertise. He enlightened me to the nuts and bolts of publishing, and doing so in a way that meets my goals as a debut author. These pages were formatted by him, according to my specifications, and were delivered promptly. The man is a pro.

I'd give a nod to my parents for always loving and believing in me, but they're both dead. Maybe they're looking down on me and smiling, but I find that idea very unsettling. When exactly are they watching me? Does no one else find this concept creepy? I'd rather just say they raised me right.

Last—and most certainly least—I want to thank everyone who ever made me feel worthless. Without you, I never would've had the ammunition to pen this narrative. With this gratitude, I implore you to look inside yourselves, and question what really prompted you to be cruel to your fellow human in those moments. I fully believe that there are no villains—everyone has a narrative that defines them. We all have a story, and we all think we're the hero in ours. Judgment, in the end, lies in whether or not we discover our own personal truths. It's a lot harder than it sounds.

ABOUT THE AUTHOR

Mark Brennan was born and raised in Cleveland, Ohio. He served five years in the Marine Corps and then attended Virginia Commonwealth University, where he attained a Bachelor of Arts degree in English. Currently, he lives in North Carolina with his wife and two children. All things considered, he's a very, very cool guy. Everyone says so.

TRIGGER/CONTENT WARNINGS

THIS STORY INCLUDES DEPICTIONS OF GUN VIOLENCE, suicide, depression, bullying, sexual assault, child abuse/neglect, and homophobic slurs.

If you or someone you know is struggling with thoughts of suicide or self-harm, all you have to do is send a text to **988** from your cell phone, or call the National Suicide Prevention Lifeline at **(800) 273-8255** (if you're not into the whole brevity thing).